For D
Max

KISSING

THE HAG

For Don +
Mae

KISSING THE HAG

BY

TIMOTHY QUIGLEY

PIXEL HALL PRESS
Newfoundland, PA USA
www.PixelHallPress.com

Kissing the Hag
by Timothy Quigley

Published by Pixel Hall Press, Newfoundland, PA USA
www.PixelHallPress.com

Printed in the United States of America

Library of Congress Control Number: 2015956964

ISBN 978-0-9860649-0-6

Publisher's Cataloging-In-Publication Data
(Prepared by The Donohue Group, Inc.)

Quigley, Timothy.
    Kissing the hag / by Timothy Quigley.

    144 pages ; cm

    Issued also as an ebook.
    ISBN: 978-0-9860649-3-7

        1. Depressed persons--Massachusetts--Boston--Fiction. 2. Homeless persons--Massachusetts--Boston--Fiction. 3. Irish Americans--Massachusetts--Boston--Fiction. 4. Storytelling--Massachusetts--Boston--Fiction. 5. Tales--Ireland. 6. Street life--Massachusetts--Boston--Fiction. 7. Urban fiction, American. I. Title.

    PS3617.I454 K57 2015
    813/.6

For Matt

At the beginning and end of this book are excerpts from *Speech from an Unfinished Play* by e.e. cummings.

This piece was submitted when the author, among other contemporary literary figures, was asked to contribute to a collection of essays, plays, fiction, and poetry titled *This Is My Best*, in 1942. When the authors were also asked to write a forward describing why the particular piece was chosen, cummings simply wrote:

"Please honor my contribution by surrounding it with a little silence. Silence is lively; deathful is double talk, eg la guerre."

"Oh my voices not all the boys who shall ever die can take you from all the girls who were ever born; and if the young moon sleeps your hands are under her sky (but without you the first star does not breath) and your fingers are walking the earth." ~ e.e. cummings

Silence...

12:38 AM

A large black woman stood outside the subway station wearing what looked like a small man's London Fog stretched tightly around her mountainous shoulders. She leaned beneath the ledge, just barely out of the rain.

"Spare any change, Mister?" she said, holding the raincoat half-closed over her wide bosom with one hand while extending the other out to me. The sleeve pulled back almost to her elbow. I just smiled, not breaking my stride. I used to give money to street people, or at least felt uncomfortable when I didn't. But now I never handed over as much as a dime. I suppose my restraint was for the same reason I didn't pray anymore. I didn't have to: When you're inside the flames that is the heart of God. The idea of petitioning Him didn't even occur to me.

Gusts of wind heaving across the empty, tree-lined pathways of Boston Common made the silvery sheet of rain sway and billow like an enormous theater curtain draped over the city. Silent, black waves rippled across the shimmering puddles that I sidestepped on my way to work at the shelter on that final night.

The evening air was cool enough to hold my breaths

in moist, dense clouds for a few seconds, just before being snatched away by another abrupt draft — gone in one swift motion, as hope is at times, or the person you once were, or believed yourself to be.

The day had gotten off to a miserable start. It had begun with brunch at the Boston Harbor Hotel with my cousin Pam, followed by a restless nap. The nap had been disrupted by another bad dream. As in so many of my dreams, my brother Mark came to me as a little kid. Only this time his face was all blue, like when I found him. I finally dozed off again and slept so deeply that when I woke up I was already twenty minutes late for work.

The Park Street Church clock was at a quarter to one as I emerged from the park. *Shit.* Forty-five minutes late, now. The tightness in my chest urged me to walk even faster.

At least it was Sunday, I reassured myself while waiting to cross Tremont. Even with the recent lifting of the blue laws that had historically kept liquor stores closed on the Lord's Day, Sunday night was still quiet at the shelter, as if all the alcoholics' internal clocks were set to skip that day. I knew that I wouldn't have to contend with so many drunks. I slid one hand high on a lamp post while waiting for a break in traffic. The wet steel was cool beneath my palm, and oddly comforting, the way a damp cloth feels to a fever.

On the opposite sidewalk, I watched my reflection pass in the dark windows of a closed Walgreen's. My hair was completely soaked, blown to the back of my head from the wind into which I was directly walking. Even in these murky shadows I looked drawn and tired. A string of cars passed and I turned to follow the slick black tires as they rolled by. I thought again of Mark's little face all blue in the dream. I tucked my hands inside the pockets of my windbreaker, clenching them into fists not quite tight enough to force the picture of him from my mind.

When I turned the corner off Church Street onto West, I saw the blue fragmented beams of a police cruiser sweeping in and out from the alleyway between the back of the old Opera House, and the crumbling Congregational church. The shelter was housed in the church's basement.

I let go of any hope for a less-than-eventful evening.

Silence...

One of the oldest congregations in Boston, the first building had burned to the ground in a fire that took the entire block in 1890. It was rebuilt almost to scale on the original brick and granite foundation.

A tin-plate photo of the old church hangs in the new church's foyer. Even beneath the yellowed matting and dusty glass it stood stoically, firmly, in solid black and white. Back then the street was lined with young trees, which I imagined had grown old and died, or had been cut down for upsetting the plumbing or pavement.

Unlike its ancestor, the contemporary church corroded along with the rest of the block; decayed and forgotten, swallowed by the steel and concrete backdrop of downtown.

In its day, the church had been postcard New England, right down to the white steeple. The upstairs, however, was much different from the Florentine regalia of the Catholic churches I had attended growing up. The walls of this church were not lined with the Stations of the Cross, nor were there any statues of saints. No angels sat on ledges, or hovered in the mid-air of murals, gesturing out toward the Holy Family in loving adoration.

None that I could see, that is.

12:54 AM

As I walked between the police car and the brick wall of the Opera House, I leaned over to see Clive Sprague sitting in the back. I knew him immediately from the faded red chamois shirt he'd worn all winter over several layers of clothes. The door was open, and he glanced at me with swollen, drunken eyes.

Relax, I told myself. *This is no big deal. The police are here all the time.*

Yeah, no big deal that they're here, while I wasn't and was supposed to be.

You blew it pal.

I squeezed between the open door and the bricks. Clive cradled one loosely bandaged hand in a bloody towel. He looked at me, and then at the towel. His pupils bobbed unsteadily in a watery pool of bright red. Not in weeks had I seen him this polluted. He'd been ill, a bad case of bronchitis that he couldn't shake.

"Figures, just figures," I groaned as I approached the commotion at the door just beyond.

There stood Claudia, a volunteer from the parish above the mission who could be a great help, really, especially at times like this when she was filling in for staff and actually pulling a shift. On the whole, though, she was hopelessly out of touch with the issue of hopelessness. I don't know. I suppose her reasons for being there were just different from mine.

She wasn't on staff, she was on the board: the only board member who attended every Tuesday's noon-toeternity staff meeting, which wouldn't have been nearly the ordeal they always were if she weren't always thinking up senseless rules. With each syllable of the point she was trying to drive home she'd tap the end of her gold Cross pen into the peeling, dark green paint on the long table we sat around in the dining hall, demanding that everyone cast their vote.

Unless, of course, it was golf or tennis season.

Right now she was bouncing up and down in the doorway, in her pink sweat suit and spotlessly white sneakers, looking as though she were warming up for a run. Her brown hair was perfectly bound in a tight ponytail that seemed never to move according to the laws of the rest of her body. Her arms were tightly folded over the word *Champion* stitched across her chest.

Hello? The Easter Bunny Hot line, please hold.

Five or six residents had gathered just behind her at the top of the stairs and were trying to peer over her pink shoulders. She was thanking the male-female team of cops, apologetically as usual. If she weren't begging your pardon for something completely out of her control, she was busy gushing over something insignificant: *'Oh that backpack is so you, where did you ever find it?'*

"Thank you. Thank you for coming so quickly," she said. "And I'm sorry, really I am, to drag you officers over here."

They both turned to walk away as I approached, looking me over in one interrogative glance, the way insufferable snobs deign to bat their eyelashes and glance sideways before dismissing you completely.

I peered sideways back at them, expressionless. Mostly, the cops treated the staff with the same distant derision they had for the residents.

Be glad we do so much of the baby-sitting for you, not to mention being a little — I don't know — grateful, maybe?

People sometimes acted as though, if the shelter

5

didn't exist, its inhabitants and their plights wouldn't either. Ignorance is piss.

Claudia began defending herself before I'd even reached the door. "I didn't know what to do. I was all alone, and he wouldn't leave. He knows he's banned for a week, Julien." Banning residents for certain infractions was one of her *rules*.

"What happened to his hand?" I asked sincerely, but meaning to sidestep any discussion on the banning policy, which I mostly ignored.

At that moment her bouncing mechanism came to a halt and her shaking mode kicked in. She stared back at me intently from inside her exaggerated shivers, looking more agitated than cold.

"He wouldn't leave," she repeated.

"What did he do to his hand?"

"He punched the wall in the common room when I told him he couldn't stay." She stepped down the two cement stairs. "He said if you were here you'd let him. That's not true! You don't let people who have been banned stay here, do you?" Her eyes narrowed on me for a few seconds, and then she cocked her chin and blinked as if I'd said: *No, I don't let them stay, but if they feel like kicking the shit out of the place, no problem.*

"Of course not," I said, already focused on those huddled in the darkness behind her. I've never had any kind of a poker face, so even this white lie was enough to make me look away.

"All right everyone, the show's over," I said to the shadows mulling around in the doorway. "Lights out in five minutes."

"Hey, we didn't get our last cigarette break," a woman's voice I didn't recognize called out from the stairwell.

I stepped out from under the floodlight hanging above the door that shone directly on Claudia. Everything beyond her and the open door was completely blocked from my view by a solid wall of black against the powerful beam.

"Yeah, we get anoth-aw butt," cried a second voice of indignation. I knew Sampson at once by the speech impediment. Then he said, "Hey Jew-ells." I had a particular affinity for Sam, but I ignored him just then. Someone else mumbled a well-rehearsed litany on personal rights.

I didn't respond to any of it, just continued to look beyond the clamor, trying to maintain a calm, level appearance. The tightness in my chest had dropped into my stomach. I waited a moment before turning back to Claudia.

"Because if you do let people who are banned stay the night," she was saying, her eyes constricting on me again, "it is a very bad thing." She gave a quick bunny shake to her head. "It is a terrible thing."

There was no chance of avoiding this discussion entirely. Still, it was time for me to assume control.

"Anyone who wants a cigarette *Goes Now*," I said into the darkness. "The door is locked and lights are out in ten minutes. And if you're left out in the alley, then you'd better have brought a blanket with you."

Claudia's invisible bunny ears twitched and grew pinker than ever. "See, this is what I mean," she said, and she threw her back against the open door while letting some of those behind file past. "The rule is: Last cigarette break at eleven o'clock."

I always tried not to find fault in the work of any of the parishioners who volunteered at the mission, as they were so greatly needed. But Claudia's pillar-of-virtue-side blocked her vision of the shelter. Your world of rules, I felt like saying, exists far beyond that door you're leaning against, not behind it. She wasn't going to be there all night like I was, hearing about the missed, and ever-popular, last cigarette break. Due to a city fire code there was no smoking in the building.

It was, of course, true that I had allowed Clive into the

shelter, even if he were banned, and anyone who came knocking on that basement door on those bitterly cold winter nights. Long after everyone else was bedded down, stragglers lay themselves to sleep a few hours by the radiator in the back hallway. In milder weather I sent them off with a blanket, or a sandwich, careful to ask if they wanted Mayo or mustard, salt or pepper. That query either got a puzzled look, or a list of special instructions. But never did I formally admit the latecomers, or readmit them as residents.

Big deal. My role was to provide shelter, not discipline. Someone beside me lit a match and the acrid puff of sulfur blew into my face before escaping on the funnel of wet wind coming up the alley.

"Have you ever filled out a Critical Incident Report?" I said to Claudia. "Have you ever *seen* a Critical Incident Report?"

"No," she said impatiently, accidentally spitting a bit as she spoke, and the tiny beads of saliva were illuminated from the light above, looking as though white sparks came lofting from her mouth. "And I don't know if I'm up to it right now, I..."

"If the police were involved, you have to. This isn't a *rule*," I said, not caring how snide I sounded, "It's the law. The incident has to be formally documented by whomever was in charge when it happened — meaning you. But I'll help."

She took a breath to speak and then stopped herself as I went past her and into the building. I knew what she was keeping herself from pointing out to me: she wouldn't have been in charge had I not been late.

As I entered the building, a strong wave of steam heat gathered all the sour odors of dirty feet and stale alcohol. Claudia followed closely behind in uncharacteristic silence. I moved quickly up the short staircase leading to the old stage that had been converted into an office for the facility.

Both of the two forward-facing desks offered a panoramic view of the entire room, which, in its day, must have played host to many pot luck dinners and bingo nights.

Now the once-open space was sectioned off by two crude, six-foot-tall partitions thrown together with unfinished drywall and two-by-fours. The walls created a corridor in the middle of the room, seven feet apart at the far end, widening to about fifteen as they approached the stage. The wide end created enough space for a common area, while the two walls transformed the long hallway into make-shift dormitories, perfectly accommodating the guests to whom it now played host.

"I was scared," she said, opening her eyes wide and throwing one hand heavily on her hip. "If a resident is a behavior problem, it's standard procedure to call the police."

Standard procedure. I took a deep breath as I leaned over the drawer of the file cabinet.

"I'm sorry you were alone, Claudia," I said. "I'm sorry Clive frightened you. And I would never criticize a judgment call you made while in charge."

"Look, I can handle this place fine," she said indignantly. "I've done it often enough."

"I'm not saying that you can't," I said. "I just hate to see the cops here at all. A lot of people in this neighborhood would like to see us shut down. You know that. And we get enough bad press without people having to read in the paper about all the stupid reasons the police..." then I caught myself. "Not that *this* is a stupid reason. I mean in general, you know?"

I searched *her* face now, and not so much for a sign of understanding, but at the very least, a pause? A flicker? Anything that would indicate less resistance.

"Where is Kevin, anyway?" I said, shuffling through the files. "He always works the Sunday night swing shift."

"He called in sick, with the flu or something." I could feel her eyes still on me.

"So I'm here alone tonight? Did anyone try to cover his shift?"

"I guess," she said, "with all that was going on... I didn't think to try and cover it."

"It's O.K. Hey," I said, looking around the room in one sweep. "It's pretty quiet in here for all the commotion, don't you think?"

"It *was* a quiet night," she said "until..."

"I know," I said sympathetically. "Look, why don't you give this a shot while I do my rounds?"

I slid the heavy drawer closed with my knee and handed her the blank form. She stared at it in one hand, and held the other out in front of her, turned up as if to ask something, but then only let out an overtly exhausted sigh.

I wanted to tell her that I really wasn't a callous person, that these so called "emergency" situations simply didn't upset me. And they wouldn't have bothered her so much if she spent more time there, whether for a paycheck *or* a bed.

She hadn't even given me a hard time for being late, yet. It was strange, almost bordering on endearing, that she seemed to be cutting me some slack.

Sometimes, when I sat up there on the old stage looking over the still sea of cots, filled with quiet breathing, I felt a deep sense of — not of authority and control, something more shepherd-like.

Or should I say, shepherd *dog*-like? That was more like it. Overseer for a few hours, and if given the opportunity, some remote type of defender, but nothing more.

More often, especially in the dark, early hours of morning, I felt the stage was actually mocking me, and I was indeed in a play. I imagined the desk lamp to be a spotlight shining on my fumbling through a script that I read like a cue card I couldn't see clearly — until too late. It was some dark comedy — way, way off-Broadway. And in the midst of every ludicrous crisis I must show where all the fragments of turmoil come dramatically together; because they actually do, at certain moments. Sometimes I even muttered stage directions to myself, which helped.

1:05 AM

"O.K.," I said under my breath as I pulled the rounds checklist from beneath the daily log, "Exit stage left." I held the clipboard in front of me and went down the four stairs leading into the rec area, and began the routine security check.

I walked slowly, referring carefully to the battered list noting different areas of the building: 1.) Alleyway. 2.) Men's Dormitory. 3) Women's Dormitory, and so on, initialing the corresponding boxes. I passed the crushed velvet reclining chair that had looked so odd to me when it was first donated a few months before. Then it was practically new — too new. Now it blended perfectly with the background, all stained in its corner of the room, its broken arm hanging limply at one side; wounded and disabled, but still functioning.

"I mean, you already have a place reserved in heaven, Jules," Pam, my cousin, had said over brunch earlier that day. "If anyone in the world knows that, I do. I mean, why are you back working at that horrid place? Don't you at least miss your old salary at the restaurant?"

Throughout the afternoon, she never stopped twisting the string of Mikimoto pearls she'd received as a wedding gift from her third set of in-laws. It wasn't too hard to remain silent. I couldn't take my mind off the light, click-clack of her meticulously French-manicured fingernails as they moved in and out among the beads.

She didn't understand that I belonged there, rather than running around at the restaurant I used to manage. She felt my skills were better served pacifying some customer whose filet mignon is taking "entirely too long" in the kitchen.

After Mark died, it had gotten to a point where I had the urge to stand in the middle of the dining room, grandly solicit everyone's attention and announce: "O.K. people, listen up. Poverty or racism or suicide would constitute a crisis situation. However, cold baked potatoes or the forgotten request for extra lemon do not. Do we understand the difference?"

Working at the shelter had been perfectly suited to my life seven years earlier. The job didn't interrupt my class schedule at Boston College, and I got all of my homework done during the graveyard shift. I'd quit drinking the year before I first worked there, so I felt as though I understood how a person could wake up one day in a world they made, but didn't necessarily choose.

This second stint at the shelter was different, though at the time of my return, I couldn't quite have articulated how. I well knew that my life had arrived at another place quite similar to the one where all the booze had deposited me — one that I didn't choose — but I wasn't aware of the comfort I drew this time around from a certain sense of belonging.

I came around the corner and stood at the head of the men's dorm, hearing the familiar creak of the side door. *Shoot.* All the doors should be locked by the time I do my first rounds.

"Can I just hold two thoughts in my head?" I said, remembering the extended cigarette break. I went toward the hallway stairs and two residents were just coming in from the alley.

"Hey," I said to Sampson and Sharon, "What's up?"

Sharon was a small woman, thin and frail, with bleached, orange hair. The skin on her face was paper thin and stretched over sharp bones. I knew she was only in her thirties, but sometimes when I looked at the way her cheeks sank, almost disappearing somewhere between her eyes and jaw I mistook her for an elderly woman.

"Nada mas, man," she mumbled as she passed, clutching a pack of Marlboros in one hand, nothing on her bony little feet but a pair of rubber thongs. Sometimes I thought of warm weather when I saw her thongs. Then I'd remember: Shit, there's snow on the ground.

"Thanks a lot. I really appreciate it," Sampson said.

He was twenty and unable to pronounce his R's. When I first met him I could hardly understand a thing he said. Now his impediment was so familiar it was unnoticeable.

"Weally apweciate?" She said, and then, "Fucking Retard," shook her head, and kept walking. Sam's face didn't register her remark. Rather, he lit up with an enthusiasm I didn't need at that particular moment.

"I missed you last night," he said. "Kevin won't play cards with me when I can't sleep. He says if I don't stay in bed all night, the next time he'll ban me. He can't, can he? He can't ban me for not sleeping, can he Julien? He can't do that, can he?"

"No," I said. "But he can ban you for being a royal pain in the ass."

Truth to tell, I really enjoyed Sampson. The way he wore me down with incessant pleading reminded me of Mark. My brother would persist until I just gave in, or used a tone in my voice that I didn't voluntarily summon. Those were the only two things that subdued him... or Sam. Mark was born just before my twelfth birthday. He was eighteen when he died.

Sampson could wear me down, and everyone else, too, and he knew it. If he didn't get what he wanted, he became belligerent, and in the presence of more than one person, he would usually create a scene.

He had a terrible mesh of twisted scar tissue from a burn that covered most of his mid- section, including his arms and hands. It was visible at the top of his chest where his flannel shirt opened, and stretched all the way around his neck. He started to rub the knotted, leathery area at his Adam's apple while his eyes shot nervously around the room. Like scribbles made with a wide Sharpie, crimson streaks blazed against the sensitive flesh of his throat. Whenever Sampson was deep in thought, or hard-pressed for an answer, he would vigorously rub his scars.

"I couldn't sleep," he said, and studied his toes as they jittered frantically at the end of his filthy, bare feet.

"I know, pal," I said, lowering my voice, going back to my list.

I had long since given up trying to make Sam sleep. Fact was I enjoyed his company on some of those late nights, when he sat up with me playing Rummy, or Fish, or his personal favorite, Old Maid. He was even a graceful loser.

Once one night, during a round of Fish, when it was his turn, he just stopped and pretended to check and rearrange his cards. He usually did this to stall when he wasn't sure of his next move, but instead of staring at the hand with his serious sort of bewilderment, he started firing questions at me about my childhood.

"What card games did you like when you were a kid? Did you have brothers and sisters? Did you get along, Jules? Did you like your teachers? Did you have a dog? I bet you had a dog. What did you name it? What movies did you like? You listened to rap I bet, I know you did, Jules."

After I slowed him down and got him to ask one question at a time, I told him everything he wanted to know, elaborating a bit here and there just to see how he grinned and buried his face behind his fan of cards in an attempt to hide his fascination. But any pauses between us were of complete ease.

"Hey Sam," I said after a quiet moment. "Since I'm spilling my life story to you, if you don't mind my asking, how did you get those scars?"

The color drained from his face as he rubbed fretfully at his throat. Immediately I wanted to take my prying question back.

"I did them myself. I was on drugs. I just did it myself," he said, one hand still at his neck and the other slowly stroking back and forth on his thigh. "On drugs. On drugs, Jules. I did it myself."

My throat closed, and I sat there for a moment at a complete loss while he slipped away from the desk and went right to bed. He didn't get up once all night.

"Is this the only way to get his ass in bed?" I ruefully asked the invisible audience.

I jammed the pen beneath the large metal clip on the board and tucked the rounds list beneath my arm, heading for the alley door. Sampson followed closely behind. "Is anyone else outside in the alley, Sam?"

"Nope, nope. Just me and Sharon, that's all that was left. Just me and her. But you know what? Guess what, you know what?"

"What Sampson? What, what?" I said, keeping my back to him, not letting him see me smile as I walked up the stairs.

"I can't sleep," he said quickly.

I stuck my head outside and looked up and down the empty alleyway. Then I slammed the heavy door shut, hard enough to engage the lock.

"What the fuck!" shouted someone from the men's side as I slid the key into the lock, turned it twice, and kicked the dead bolt over with my foot.

"Can't a person get a freaking' night's sleep in this

hole?"

"Will you all just shut the fuck up!" bellowed a woman's voice.

"You can't sleep, aye?" I asked Sampson. "You haven't even undressed yet, pal. You can't tell me that you've even tried."

I went back to the list — everything cool here, check — and walked toward the men's dorm with Sam on my heels.

"Do you want to play rummy with me tonight, huh? Do you want to play fish?" I knew he was trying to grease me by not mentioning Old Maid.

"Sampson, no. What I want you to do is get into bed and stay there." I wanted him to at least go and lie down for now.

"Do you want to see my new cards?" he said. "I got a new deck just for us. Just for you and me."

"No Sam, not now. Bed. Now. Bed."

Walking away he slapped the bottoms of his feet on the cement floor, mumbling: "Asshole, cocksucker," to himself.

"Come here, you little rodent," a voice from the men's side said, "and let me make that same noise on your head." Then a boot came flying at Sampson's back, just missing him.

"Easy!" I shouted into the dimly lit room.

Oh man, no more scenes tonight, please. I knew just who the voice belonged to, *and* the boot: Winston Walker, classic son of a bitch.

I spun around and bent over the foot of his bed. If I were any closer at that moment I could have seized him by the throat. "Winston, you freakin' settle down, or..." I stopped.

"Look," I reasoned, with great strain. "Just cool it, O.K.? Everyone wants to sleep, right?"

Relax, I told myself. *He's just a drunk.*

But Winston wasn't even liked by his fellow alcoholics. He never shared his booze, and he was a thief, breaking probably the only two codes of honor around there. He sat upright in his bed, pointing a shaking hand at me.

"Why don't you do your job and keep this place in fucking order? You're all such fucking idiots. Why don't you just throw that retarded pain in the ass out in the rain?"

Sam smiled, but nervously, as if he were about to laugh. But I knew it was to mask something like shame, but different. Mark had had almost the very same self-conscious smile — only all of the time. But I never saw it as embarrassment. It seemed more bashful, as if something unseen were accidentally being revealed about him.

"Hey, listen Walker," I said. "If there were a law against retards then I wouldn't be in here either," I said.

I must be retarded.

He lay down again, saying what a stupid bastard I was, while some other guy near him yelled, "This place is a God-damned nut house."

"Got that right, buddy," I whispered, glancing up the row of beds, and back down to the clipboard.

Everything cool here, for all intents and purposes. Check.

As soon as I came around the corner to the women's side, there was Rosie sitting on her bed, waiting for me as always. Always, that is, if she were not on some city bench sleeping off a bottle or three of Wild Irish Rose.

"Hello Darlin'," she said through a wine-soaked brogue. "Would they be giving you a bit of grief over there?" She was about seventy; her face puffy and smooth with one eye permanently closed.

"Oh just a bit," I said. "How are you doing? You didn't come back Thursday night, and I was... wondering about you."

I was careful not to say: worried.

"Oh, the weather was so pleasant for once I thought

I'd have myself a holiday," she said.

What she meant was she'd passed out under a night sky beneath which it was mild enough to sleep it off. If she weren't unconscious somewhere, she was selling balloons on The Common, or cruising around downtown tanked up on cheap wine, managing to bend someone's ear. She was a sweet woman, and possessed enough quick charm in her one eye to win over many passing strangers. The drunker and crazier Rosie acted, the more people loved her — even when she argued quite loudly on city sidewalks with her unseen angels. But no one took her seriously. *Having a holiday.*

"Oh, vacationing in The Public Garden are we then, Miss Rosie?" I said affecting my own lame attempt at a brogue.

"I was just fine," she said, and peered off vacantly over my head, as she always did when beginning to discuss her angel. "Don't ever waste your time worrying for this one. I'm always very well taken care of, you know that."

It sounded very personal when she said "you know that."

Despite all her years of heavy boozing, she was, at times, more perceptive and lucid than just about anyone I've ever known drunk or sober.

Rosie talked about angels all the time, and I always listened with great care.

"She takes very good care of me," she said, still looking past me as if some divine, ethereal being hovered just above my head. "I might have been on a little tear there, but did you hear what happened?"

"What?"

"You mean to say that you didn't hear what happened Friday, then?"

"No," I said, "I was off yesterday and I took Friday off because I wasn't feeling…" I hesitated, "that well. What happened?"

"I just came home without my teeth is all," she said with a smile and a rise to her brow that suggested something pleasant about this revelation. She opened her mouth wide so I could see her smooth, bare gums. A fusty whiff of vinegary wine and tobacco made me stop breathing through my nose and pull back a bit.

"Oh, Rosie," I said. "It's going to be another year to get those replaced."

"It would be, Mr. Julien, but slow down now. Do you discern so much as a drop of worry in this eye?" She leaned toward me and pulled down at her open eyelid with one wavering index finger. Then she faltered a bit more forward than she expected, and unsteadily reached for the blue plastic cup beside her bed.

"They're right herie, dearie," she said, her words still staggering sluggishly together from her last drunk. "I woke in the middle of the night and found them right here."

"And?" I said.

"And what, Mr. Julien?"

"And who got them to you?"

"You know very well who got them to me."

"Your cop-angel," I said, "or angel-cop, whichever came first."

"You know, she sees to it that I get what I need. Kevin said somebody dropped them off." She stopped, and looked directly at me. "But what does that prove?"

"Oh, like he would know an angel if it appeared in a pool of white light and started to pluck her harp with his nose," I said.

She laid one smooth, warm hand on my arm. I sat perfectly still. I wanted to ask her how she knew her angel was a girl, and what was the sound of her voice, but I had to get back to Claudia before she suffered an aneurysm over that report.

"Cigarette break, later?" I whispered, and patted two fingers lightly against my lips as I stood.

"Oh, I'll be up for a while yet. I've slept most of the day." She covered her mouth in a girlish way as if she were giggling, but no sound came out. In moments like this, I would imagine Rosie as a little girl, her laughter rising through the thatched roof of a small stone cottage, in the village of her Irish childhood.

Silence...

1:27 AM

I could hear my boss' voice coming from the office as I came around the corner of the women's area.

Why is Kyle here? I wondered, and reminded myself that he was not only the director of the shelter, but the minister of the church as well. He could be here for anything.

I headed up the aisle to the stage.

Kyle looked up from the desk where he was hunched over while helping Claudia with the report. He had a concentrated look that didn't relax at all when his eyes fell on me. He said nothing, and I took the long way around.

"O.K., enter stage right," I said softly, ascending the short stairs.

"Hey Kyle," I said, trying not to sound as edgy as I felt, and sat at the desk opposite him. I shuffled around and pretended to look for something on top.

I felt him watching me, waiting a moment before he simply said, "Julien," then focused back on the report.

I filed all the day's paperwork and read the log twice. Then I folded my hands in front of me and stared down intently, pretending to be deep in thought; exactly the same posture I'd assumed for most of the afternoon with Pamela.

"You can't just thrust yourself into purgatory," was one of the fine pearls of wisdom she dropped just before we parted. "You can't blame yourself for Mark's death."

I had sat perfectly still in the hotel dining room, staring down at my hands folded on the table. I thought of how much Mark's hands had resembled my own — and how much they were like our father's. Mark would hold his up to mine every now and then and remark how similar they were. "Look," he'd say, as if he'd only just noticed. "They're just like mine."

An older black man approached the stage. He had a red bandana folded and tied around his forehead. Something stuck up from just above his left ear that looked like an Indian's feather. When he got closer I could see it was a cross made from two weathered Popsicle sticks, wrapped tightly in the center with a shoelace. When he got to the stage, he started going on about having arrived earlier in the evening and not receiving any linen. He was speaking low and quite fast, a kind of babbling undertone.

"Slow down, pal. What bed are you in?" I'd never seen him before.

"Seventeen, brother," he said, and smiled, showing an uneven row of caramel-colored teeth.

I reached for the bed chart and ran my finger down to seventeen. "Preacher Jack?" I said a bit too loudly, and both Claudia and Kyle looked up from the report.

"Yes brother," the man said. "Praise Jesus."

He followed me to the laundry area on the far wall between the dorms where I handed him a clean set of faded, mismatched sheets. "Please put them here in the morning," I said motioning to the hamper in the corner. It was the large, cloth kind on wheels you see in the corridors of hospitals and hotels.

"I know, brother. What's yo' name?"

"Julien. How do you know where anything goes?" I asked. "Have you ever stayed here before?" I could never be too suspicious of drifters.

"No," he said, "but I stayed in enough like it. They's lots a things Preacher Jack knows. Lots a things Preacher Jack sees."

"Oh yeah?" I said, "Like what?"

He turned his head and cupped a hand over the side of his mouth so I couldn't see his lips, and whispered something low and inaudible into an imaginary ear. Then he shrugged his shoulders at his invisible friend and turned back to me.

"I'm not wastin' my time on you. I think you know," he said, and looked at me long and confidently.

"Yeah, yeah," he said in a taunting voice as if I *denied* it. "You know already, or you pretty close to knowin'. Preacher Jack can always tell who knows and who needs to know. It's in the eyes, brother. Always in the eyes."

Always in the eyes.

I came around from the men's dorm just as Kyle was rising from the desk. I could have done that report with Claudia in three minutes. He still had his coat on; I hoped that was a good sign.

"Can I see you in my office for a moment, Julien, please?" he said before I'd reached the stairs.

"Sure," I said.

Fuck. He can't be firing me. I work a million hours for him. Besides, he likes me.

I so wished to be back in my apartment. I just wanted to be home.

His office was a small room off the hallway behind the stage leading to the kitchen and dining hall. It was always musty in there, the damp air preserving the stuffy odor. It reminded me of a warehouse or garage. Two chairs faced one another in front of the gray metal desk — an old, overstuffed armchair covered with a brown-and-orange afghan; and a scratched-up maple rocker. The wall behind the desk was covered with mostly yellowed, but some newer, liberal political cartoons and clippings. A bumper sticker on the front of the desk read SHELTER THE HOMELESS, NOT NUCLEAR WARHEADS.

Kyle sat in the rocker, and motioned me to the

armchair.

Oh, please, let this be quick.

"Julien," he said, "you know how much I appreciate the job you do around here, as much as I enjoy knowing you personally."

What the hell else can I do for money if I can't even do this? I closed my eyes tightly in response to the invisible nail pounding through the front of my skull.

"Are you all right?" he asked, and I looked up as if I'd missed something.

"No. I mean... yes. Yes, I'm fine. I'm just tired," I said. "I haven't been feeling all that well —."

"Do you think you've been working too much?" he said, tilting his head forward, looking over the wire rims of his glasses.

"Well, I've had the last two days off and I'm feeling pretty well rested," I said with a pause.

How contradictory is that? I hoped he wouldn't pick up on it, and counted the white rings of water stains fanning out over the small, wooden end table between us. There were seven.

"How is everything else?" he asked. Kyle never played minister with me, out of mutual respect, I supposed. He was the only person at the shelter who knew about Mark aside from Rosie, but he never brought it up and I appreciated that. But it was clear at the moment what he meant by "everything".

"How's your family doing?"

"They're fine, everything's fine."

He waited, giving me the opportunity to say something more.

"Well I have to tell you," he began again, "though I feel completely confident when you are here running things — that in itself, isn't enough."

"Look Kyle," I said, "I've been feeling a bit burnt out, it's just that..."

"Julien," he stopped me. "Eh… It just isn't fair to the person you're relieving when you're late. You know there should be two staff members here during peak times."

"I didn't know Kevin wasn't here," I said.

"Claudia tried to call you…" he said, and then let that statement trail off as we had this conversation before. In the last year I had pretty much kept the ringer off most of the time, then stopped answering it altogether.

"The fact is," he said continuing, "you should have been here long before the police were."

"I'm sorry," I said directly to his face, and then away, "I overslept." It sounded like a confession.

Where the hell am I?

"Sorry isn't good enough, Julien," he said, and the well of dread deepened in my stomach. "I'm not going to be able to tolerate it any more after tonight."

After tonight?

"Is it true you let guests stay here who have been banned?"

"No," I said, trying to act surprised at the accusation, yet feeling as though I'd been caught in a lie and hoping it didn't show on my face. "Once or twice I've let Clive or George Douglas in during a blizzard maybe, to sit for a while in the hallway. What's the big deal?"

"It's a big deal when we aren't consistent. Letting someone in from the cold is not the end of the world, but what's this about the bathroom door locks?"

"What's what?" I said, thinking, *I knew this would haunt me. Why tonight?*

"You know they're supposed to be locked at all times. Have you been leaving them unlocked on your shift?" I did not want to answer this question.

The locked bathrooms were a new rule, one of Claudia's ideas to curb cigarette smoking in them. Not only did guests resent having to ask to use the bathroom all the time, but it was a huge drag for me to play "keeper of the key" all night. Besides, I didn't really care if someone grabbed a butt or two in the middle of the night. A lot of those who wanted a smoke were jonesing for something worse.

"Sometimes it's not really necessary."

"Indeed it is!" he said. I was startled. I hadn't expected him to cut me off again. "People *have* been smoking in the bathrooms, and not only that, it makes other staff members look like the bad guys. It *will* stop tonight. What I'm saying is that we all need to be working together here. All on the same page, do you understand?" He was looking over his glasses again, and I rubbed my forehead to signal my consideration of all he was saying.

"You have to act like you work here as part of a team," he said, "not as though you run the place yourself. Do something to show me you know what I mean, O.K.?"

His face had become stiff and unsympathetic, an expression I had seen on his face only when he was looking at some of the characters who sometimes came around here causing trouble. This was worse than getting fired. I had never imagined how it would be to see him look at me like that.

"If it's a matter of cutting back your hours some, I can do that." It sounded like an ultimatum and I think he knew that was how I understood it. He waited a moment, then said, "What I mean is, that it's not a problem. You just need to let me know what's going on."

"No, no. I'll be fine," I said, "I'll be O.K." I really was at a loss. The phone on his desk started ringing, but he ignored it. The two of us fell silent, and the pauses between rings seemed immense.

The phone stopped.

"This isn't the first time we've had this discussion Julien," he said, more gently, but speaking carefully, "though it will be the last."

There were two quick knocks on the door and Claudia

stepped in the room.

"Excuse us, Claudia," Kyle said, "Will you give us a few minutes?"

"Sorry," she said flatly. "Telephone, Julien, it's your brother," she said. She looked only at Kyle, then closed the door.

Carey was probably the last person I wanted to talk to at that moment. "I'm going to take it in here if you don't mind," I said.

"All right. Don't forget to lock the door. Have a good shift." He stood and zipped his coat, "And please," he said, "think about what I've said."

"Yes," I said. "I will." I think I was more embarrassed than anything else. Clearly, Claudia had rung him at home. That was why she never mentioned my tardiness. She knew that I was getting my butt chewed, too, but she barged right in as if she had every right to because she had blown the whistle on me.

"Tell Claudia I'll be out in a minute," I called as he left, though I was thinking: *She can wait all night.*

I held the receiver to my ear, but watched the red light blink several times before pressing it.

1:59 AM

"This is Julien," I said — as if I didn't know who was on the other end.

"Yeah, it's me," Carey said through the static of his cell phone. "Where the hell have you been?"

I huddled over on the desk, my face only a few inches from the faded blotter. "What do you mean?" I said, annoyed. "Here. Home. Nowhere."

Carey didn't speak for a moment. He was in his car and I heard the DJ announcing a new song.

"Mom was expecting you for dinner this afternoon."

"Shit." I bolted upright in the chair.

"You told me you'd come. She cooked a roast." The music had started and muffled some of the agitation in his voice

"I told you that I *could* make it…" I said, and then stopped, realizing he was right.

"I said I'd pick you up," he said. "I rang your bell for a half-hour. Were you just ignoring me?"

"No, no," I said, now beginning to piece together the conversation we had three days before. "I was out with Pam. We had brunch. I'm sorry. I completely spaced."

The music in his car was unexpectedly silenced. "Bullshit, Julien."

"No, really," I said. "Pam's been…"

"Pam has nothing to do with it. You would've been there if you wanted to. It's bad enough that you dick me around all the time, but do you have to treat Mom that way?"

"What the hell are you talking about?" I said, knowing exactly what he meant. Carey was three years younger than me. *I* was the big brother, and whenever he tried to dispense castigation or even unsolicited advice, I immediately became incensed. It didn't matter if he knew what he was saying.

"You should have seen her... Sitting at the dining room table, with only me and the roast," he said. "She even made broccoli casserole, and twice-baked potatoes. She looked so sad." And then in a quieter, more wistful voice, "Disappointed, really."

"Oh God," I said, moving the receiver away from my chin. My family seemed incredibly small at that moment, as if I had been looking at them through the wrong end of a telescope.

"Are you there?"

I let my head drop and shook it. "Yeah, yeah, I'm here."

"You've got to get it together, man."

"What do you mean?" I said, really meaning it.

"Mom's worried about you, and she doesn't need anything else to worry about, you know?"

Oh good. Now I'm losing my foothold in the family, too.

It wasn't only sibling rivalry that let him get to me so when he told me off. It also recalled, all too well, the time when my life was at its bottom, and didn't warrant much respect. In those days, the older brother protocol vanished along with any semblance of control and self-esteem. I felt just then as if the same were happening again.

"Hey, since when the hell are you *Mr. I'll-keep-everyone-together,* huh?" I said. "When have you ever had to take care of anyone but yourself?"

"Fuck you. I don't even know why I called..." he

said, sounding a bit injured instead of pissed off.

"Yes, you do," I said. "You wanted to make me feel like shit." When it came to getting what he wanted, Carey had the same power over me Mark had had. Only Carey used guilt.

"Oh, here we go," he said, all confidence back. "I'm not getting on that bus with you, Jules. I just wanted you to know that mom wants to talk to you about Mark's memorial Mass. She wants to have people back to the house after, for breakfast, or coffee, or whatever."

I imagined my mother's house filled with people — but empty.

Silence...

As I go down my mother's street, I look around me and say, "This is where my brother walked, the pavement he moved over. His head and shoulders rose above the line of these hedges, as he came around this corner."

And as I approached her door I'd say, "These are the stairs he ascended for the last time, that day...'"
Where was I?

The house in which we grew up was a big, old brownstone on Commonwealth Avenue, in between Berkley and Clarendon. If you came in the front door, which we were never allowed to use as children, you faced a staircase that stopped at a small landing three quarters of the way down, and turned toward you. The landing was exposed on all sides, and from the front door you could look across the living room, and then over an old mahogany dry bar you could see into the kitchen beyond. Pine beams framed the ceilings and were stained light maple to match the large window seat in the kitchen. It had forty-six panes and, in throes of torment and distress, I washed every one of them, inside and out, along with the other kitchen windows, every

Saturday morning, for years.

Before my parents remodeled, the forty-six panes were just two ordinary kitchen windows. In front of them stood the dressing table used for changing Carey. I remember standing on a chair beside my father as he gave Carey a clean diaper. He was in boxer shorts with no tee shirt. I remember watching the muscles in his chest rise and constrict tensely with each attempt to push the large safety pins through the thick, white cotton, and how Carey screamed if accidentally pricked.

It was a window seat by the time Mark was born, though still the baby station. I was changing the diapers by then, and fortunately Pampers with tape were on the market. It was around that time that I started noticing my father being gone for days at a time and knowing that he actually *wasn't* "away on business."

I would stand at that window seat and look at my reflection broken into several, small rectangular pieces, and say, "See. Nothing really is changed. Everything looks different, but it's just the same. Nothing's changed."

2:08 AM

"I'll call her tomorrow," I said.

"Yeah, please do."

I let out a long, deep breath, holding the receiver away from my face.

"You know," he said, "you talk to me as if whatever I have to say isn't even valid. All my life I've never been able to tell you a God-damned thing."

"Oh, here we go," I said. "Do you have your little Rolodex of resentments in front of you?"

"Forget it Julien, I have to go."

"No… you forget it. Do you think I don't know what Mom's been through?"

"Just drop it," he said. "Forget I said anything."

"Since when do you put a cap on conversations with me? Huh?" I said, realizing that I was beginning to yell.

"Drop it Julien," he said more loudly this time, over me. It was as though my head were being held under water. I waited before I said, "Look, Carey, guess what? I'm at work now and I…"

"Yeah, I know. I called you there, remember? Speaking of which, I was at your old job with people from work — at the bar, that is. Anyway, I ran into the owner. What is her name again?

"Terry?"

Yes, that's her. Anyway, she was behind the bar doing inventory or something and recognized me from going in there when you managed the place. She told me to tell you that your old job is still waiting for you, whatever that means."

"Whatever that means?"

"Yeah, whatever, Jules. Just thought I'd pass it along. Look, call Mom. She's worried."

I slammed my free hand on the desk. "Why is everyone so God-damned worried? I'm doing fine. Tell her I'm fine."

"You tell her."

"*You,*" I said, and then stopped, imagining what we sounded like.

"Julien, *please?*" He said, sounding so distressed, it was as if *he* were in trouble.

"What?" I said, but patiently this time.

"I feel like I'm losing you, Jules. I don't know. I'm just really scared all of the time, and I don't know why."

"That's nonsense." I didn't know what else to say. "I'm right here."

"Just call Mom, all right?"

"All right," I said, surprised by my complete surrender and the tone of reassurance in my own voice. "I will. I promise. But listen, Pal: Don't worry. Everything is going to be all right. We're going to be fine, O.K.?"

He was silent.

"And I'll call you tomorrow," I said.

"Yeah, right," he said over a car's horn booming in the background.

"No, really. I've got to go now, but I will. I promise."

"You better."

I hung up the phone.

I held my head and pressed my fingers against my temples, still stuck with the image of my mother at the dining room table.

I could see her face vividly — its weary, defeated look. Every time I saw that expression, it made me consider all the times I had been the cause of it.

Silence…

When I opened my eyes in the Intensive Care Unit of Mass. General, I vaguely recalled the ambulance ride as traces of bright lights and shiny, gleaming objects, shadowy figures hovering over me and moving quickly.

What I didn't recall was the six hours of surgery it took to repair my wrist, or the day, or the time, or even the events leading me to the ambulance ride and the hospital bed.

"Good afternoon."

I had thought I was alone. My mother's voice startled me. I looked about and saw her in a chair by the foot of the bed, set back against the window in the nook where the closet ended. A slant of soft light from the hallway stretched across her shoulders and head. She sat perfectly straight, waiting. She was staring, but not at me, just into the room. Her vacant look transcended anger, even hurt. It was desolate.

I turned over, facing the wall, cringing from the knowledge that the desolation was because of *me* — and that it had been there throughout my plunge into alcoholism.

"I did it because I wanted the pain to stop—for *everyone*," I mumbled to the wall.

Who was Mark sparing?

"How could you possibly think *that*," she said in a very low voice that sounded almost cruel. She took a deep breath, and I turned to look at her.

"You are my first born, Julien, my miracle. I *dreamed* you. I remember the first time I felt you move inside me." She put her hand on her belly, and let out a sob, a single, deep gasp.

"I created you," she said. "Fuck you."

A woman began to scream somewhere on the same floor.

It had been so long since I'd been able to shed a tear that I didn't notice the thickening in my throat, the light spasms in chin and lips. Again, I rolled away, to face the wall.

"Even Jesus wept, for Christ's sake," she said. "You think you're so strong, but you're not. You're just foolish. And human, like everyone else — though at the rate you're going, probably not for long."

The only other sound in the room was the soft, steady bleep of the heart monitor. Then, the woman down the hall started screaming again. Only this time her cries crescendo into a banshee-like wail reverberating down the hallway. My mother reached over to hold my hand briefly, then, without saying anything else, left the room.

For the rest of my time in that bed, between intervals of restless sleep, and doctors and nurses coming and going, I lay there wondering: *How did I end up here? Was there some defining moment of passage, or a single choice?*

I could never bear going to Mark's grave with my mother. I carried his death around with me, but at the cemetery this became all too apparent, as if the rest of the world were only a backdrop, and my mother just a prop standing beside the black, polished granite bearing his name. She had faced his suicide squarely — joined support groups, started a scholarship fund, spoke of him and *it* often — but she never cried over it, not that I ever saw. And not because she couldn't. It was as if she wanted to keep her tears to herself as a way of keeping her youngest son near her as well. Seeing that was every bit as heartbreaking as seeing his name on the gravestone.

I would endure many sleepless nights in the months after Mark died, before I came back to work at the shelter, and this was many years after that time in the ICU. But I was still asking myself the same question: *How had I gotten here?* I'd thought I had already sunk as low as the human spirit possibly could. But I came back — then. *What was this new place?*

How could everything spiral so completely out of my control, again? As if it were never in my control at all. The part of me that was Mark was gone. It was as if the person I was: The *brother* I was, had been rendered null, all previous meaning swept away; lost, like confidence, or faith; as if vanished in one abrupt act of betrayal.

Of what worth was a lifetime of being a good brother if it was all to end with waking up one day and realizing you were wrong about everything?

Silence...

2:11 AM

Claudia had her coat on, and was sitting on one of the desks, checking her make up in a compact mirror.

"I have to go now," she said.

"Don't let me keep you," I quipped. "Oh, sorry," I added. "That call was kind of important."

"Well?" she said, as if expecting me to say something more. Then, she snapped the compact shut and dropped it in her purse. "Whatever. You have a good shift, now," she said, not even hinting at sincerity, and left.

"I will, *now*," I muttered to the echo of her footssteps making their way up the stairs to the alley door, and grabbed a paperback copy of *The Great Gatsby* with heavily creased pages and no cover. I'd set it aside from one of the donation boxes the week before. Soon I was lost in the excesses and decadence of the Roaring Twenties.

2:47 AM

The ringing of the telephone echoed in the tall space between me and the ceiling. I started at first, then stared at the receiver as the ringing continued. All I needed was another phone conversation like the one with Carey. Worst case scenario: Yet another family member? Who now? My father? Daddy-o, just dropping a dime in the middle of the night?

"Hello?"

"Is, ah, Juan there?" some Spanish dude said, then hung up.

I laughed at myself for imagining it was my old man, though that would've been precisely his MO. Out of the blue, he'd find me and engage in a round of emotional and mental torture, if only for the fun of it, but it was always the same.

The telephone had wakened me from a sound sleep. I remember grabbing the receiver from beside my bed and holding it to my ear without opening my eyes.

"Hello?"

"Duke?"

"Dad?"

"The Duke!" he said, the nickname he'd given me in honor of his all-time hero, John Wayne. I liked it when I was small. When I got older, I'd think: *How can a movie star be anyone's hero? They aren't even themselves.*

"What are you doing?" he said, slurring a bit. He tried to speak slowly and carefully enunciate his words whenever he was drunk. Who did he think he was fooling?

"It's eight-fifteen, Dad. What do you think I'm doing?"

"Well, I thought I might have missed you — that you'd be off to your Chef's duties at the yacht club."

Chef's duties. How grandiose. Everything with him was subject to hyperbole.

"I'm the *assistant* chef, Dad. Let me translate: I'm a cook." I imagined the dumbfounded expression on his face just then, and wished I hadn't said it.

"Anyway, the dining room is closed on Mondays." I almost added that it was also the only day I could sleep-in.

"Well, I didn't mean to bother you." He said it so politely I actually felt sorry for him. I always did at first whenever we met or spoke — random meetings punctuating stretches of absence — years, to be precise.

"You're not bothering me. It's just that, well, I haven't heard from you in, what is it, almost two years? Then, you just call out of the blue, wake me up, and ask me what I'm doing.

"Sorry. I was just thinking about you, and being right nearby…"

Oh great. Classic Daddy-O. You don't see or hear from him since the last presidential administration, then he appears out of nowhere, without warning, or tact, on your front porch, or at your job. Always on impulse, and always tanked.

The last time I'd seen him was at Verve, a French restaurant on Newbury Street where I'd waited tables a few years. I came around the corner to the bar and there he was, white hair a wind-blown nest on top of his head, face pale and chapped.

He leaned crookedly against one of the stools, one foot on one of the rungs in a pathetic attempt to steady himself. He was wearing a tee shirt and a V-neck sweater beneath a worn, tweed blazer, buttoned too tightly around his swelling gut. On his feet were boat shoes without socks, a fashion flashback to his preppie youth. He never wore socks with Topsiders, even during the years when he was well dressed and groomed.

Back then, he wore a suit every day, and a black cashmere overcoat that made him look quite distinguished, especially when his hair began to turn white prematurely, at first with a light covering of frost at the temples.

Booze had taken everything from him: His family, his business, his class. He was now just a drunk.

Leaning there in the crowded bar among the Back Bay's urban-arty crowd, he looked like a panhandler who'd wandered in off the street.

I made a beeline for him. Teeth clenched, my face only inches from his, I growled at him: "What the hell are you doing here?"

"I was just thinking about you."

"No," I said. "I'm busy," and grabbed him by the arm. Hoping no one would notice, or see any resemblance, I ushered him through the cocktail lounge.

Then he stopped mid-way and I slammed right into him, practically knocking him over. My hand tightened on his arm and I pulled him back toward me.

"Oh, come on now," he said. "I don't want a drink. I just wanted to see you."

"No," I said in a voice I'd use scolding a child. "You can't just come here like this."

Two women from a gallery up the street were seated at a small table beside us. They looked up from their bottle of Merlot, and stopped talking. Oh great, I thought, they're in here every day.

The one with red hair was quite a bit older than the other, and always wore brown lipstick. She squinted at me. She had on a carved wooden elephant necklace with large, angular beads. From that day on I noticed it every time she wore it.

I turned him around. "You can't just come in here," I said again, and led him through the crowd. The early evening set was mostly comprised of commuters killing rush-hour over tall, frosty pints of micro-brews, or designer martinis served straight up in chilled, fluted glassware. Fortunately no host was at the front.

He stopped again in the foyer, and started, "I was…"

"No," I said, louder this time, and he shrank away from my voice, hunching his shoulders a bit. At times like this, he might as well have driven a bolt through the left side of my chest. But nothing could quell the rage he inevitably sparked in me. And as soon as I caught myself feeling any sympathy for him, I'd remember everything.

How he left my mother with nothing but debts. How she went back to work at the bank, and afterward straight to night classes at Northeastern. How there was never enough money, and how he never forked over as much as a dime. I had to pay my last year of tuition at Gov. Bullfinch's myself. I got a reduced fee, and I wasn't too timely on the payments, but no one ever hassled me. It was either that, or finish up at a public school. In the meantime, I worked weekends at a restaurant and watched my brothers during the week while my mother worked and went to school.

Old Daddy-O was never around, except for brief appearances as when he'd promise to chaperone one of Mark's field trips. The Science Museum outing was a beauty. First, he failed to meet the kids at the school. Poor Mark just assumed he'd been blown off. Then, he shows up at the museum completely sloshed an hour after Mark's third grade class had arrived there.

I stood in the foyer of the restaurant as he walked up the steps to the street. When he got to the top he stopped on the corner and attempted to smooth down his hair in the wind gusting up Exeter Street. He stood still for a few moments, then looked around, trying to decide whether to go right or left — or maybe he just couldn't see how the streets intersected at all, but rather how they had led to where he now stood — this point of impasse.

"So you're right nearby, are you?" I said into the phone, sitting up and throwing my legs over the side of the bed, opening my eyes slowly, letting them adjust to the morning sun. I envisioned him outside on the sidewalk, staring up at the windows of my third-floor apartment.

"Where are you?"

"Union Street," he said. "Just downtown."

Union Street. Great. Nothing closer to skid row north of Boston. I could hear the faint rumble of traffic in the background, louder at times, accompanied by an occasional screech that I imagined was the swinging door of some dive in Central Square.

"What do you say, Duke? How about you come and meet your old man for a beer?"

"It's not even 8:30."

"Oh," he said, and was silent.

"Besides," I said, "I don't drink anymore. I haven't for over a year."

"Well, you're a better man than I am, Gunga Din," he said, straining a husky, haggard laugh into the phone. But I knew he meant it.

"Do you know what I'm going to do today, son?"

"I know one thing. You won't be coming to see me if you're smashed."

"I'm not smashed," he said. "And I know just what I'm doing."

"And what might that be?"

"I'm going to kill myself."

"Knock it off!" I said in my scolding-the-child-voice.

"No, no, it's true," he said. "I just want you to remember one thing for me."

"Dad, will you cut the drama, please, I…"

"Just remember I wasn't always such a bad guy," he

said.

"I'm not going to need to because…" But he'd already hung up.

What was I supposed to do, pull the covers over my head and go back to sleep?

I got dressed, and went downtown to look for him. I didn't think I would find him, and I didn't. It was just like when I was ten, and he'd disappear for days on end. He'd be off on a bender, and I'd be walking around the school yard, thinking: *He's dead. He's somewhere dead.*

On the way home, I rented some DVDs and sat on the couch into the night, unable to concentrate. I was watching this movie about the making of another movie, and I got totally lost. I had to keep rewinding it. The phone was between me and the TV and I kept shifting my attention between it and the screen.

I expected it to ring again, but it never did. That's how it is with drunks. They'll drive you insane long before they ever bottom out themselves. They're always fine in the end, most of the time. My old man was, anyway. I can't say as much for myself.

Seven months later, he showed up at the yacht club as I was coming in for my shift. He was just sitting there, reading a newspaper, settled quite comfortably in one of the over-stuffed easy chairs in the lobby, just like he belonged there. He'd grown a beard and wore an Irish knit turtleneck he probably thought made him look like Hemingway. To me, he looked more like Foster Brooks, but at least he wasn't drawing any attention.

Close-up, his eyes seemed relatively clear, his face fuller than it had looked in years. I figured he'd been drying out in some detox, or holding tank, hence the beard.

He put the paper down and smiled. "The Duke!" he said. His over-emphatic delivery made plain he was back on the sauce.

"Hey," I said flatly, shifting the backpack on my shoulder.

"What's in the bag? Looks heavy."

"Books," I said.

"Books!" he said. "Why are you carrying them around?" He stood carefully, and then gave me a light jab on the arm with a closed fist. "Did you jog here with them on your back for a little workout?"

"Ha. Funny," I said. "I just came from school."

"School?"

"Yeah, it's where one goes to better oneself, Dad," I said. He fiddled with the paper while unsuccessfully trying to fold it neatly, and then added it to a pile on the table beside him. His hands were shaking, and I could smell gin.

"I'm in my second year at Bunker Hill Community. I'm hoping to transfer to Boston College next year and finish my bachelor's."

"Your bachelor's?" he said, shaking his head.

"B. A. in business? What part are you missing? Oh, I'm sorry," I said and put my hand up to my forehead, "That would be the last decade."

"No, no, no," he went on like I was straying from the topic. "What about Chef's School?"

"Chef's School?" I said. "I don't want to go to Chef's School."

"But didn't you already go? Duke?"

"No, Dad."

I could just see him on some bar stool, bragging to some poor schlep about his son, The Chef. La-di-fucking-da. "That's my Duke. Went to Chef's school. Always a go-getter, that one." He'd probably go on to say how he got me interested in cooking because in the Navy he'd been the third cook to the Admiral's second-best shoe shine boy, or some such crap. The story might eventually get back to me.

Thinking about his lies, and how he actually seemed to believe them, I always felt sad at first. But then I remembered how little he actually knew about me, and how much he made up.

What little sympathy I had left for him dissolved when he started again with the "Duke" business.

"And cut the Duke-shit," I said. "What do you want? Were you just *thinking* about me, like when you called me last November?"

"When?" he said, and ran his fingers over the ribbed collar of his sweater. He didn't know what I was talking about.

"I gotta go," I told him, and for a moment he looked genuinely surprised. Only for a moment. Then he looked down at his shoes and scraped one foot over the other, pretending to wipe off a smudge on the leather, or something.

"Last time we spoke you were about to commit suicide," I said. "How did that turn out?" He didn't even bother to look up. I turned toward the dining room.

Four years passed before I saw or spoke with my father again. Not until the morning after I found Mark. I was sitting at the kitchen table in my aunt's house, and he walked into the room so nonchalantly you'd have thought he lived next door. Mercifully, he was in pretty good shape. He had a fresh haircut and was wearing a navy blue cashmere sweater that at least looked new. One of his brothers had probably taken him shopping and to a barber that very morning. He sat down at the table with me, Carey, Pam, and my Aunt Maureen, as we waited for Mom's plane to land at Logan.

She'd been down in North Carolina attending the wedding of a friend's son. A few months later she told me how, as the plane was preparing to land, a terrible chill came over her. She shook so badly that the flight attendant got her a blanket. She said she sat there, unable to get warm, wishing the plane would just keep circling the airport and never land.

Ladybug, ladybug, fly away home. Your house is on fire, your children are alone.

My mother's sister lived just off Copley Square on Saint Batolph Street, two blocks from where my father had grown up. He sat with his hands folded in front of him on the worn Formica table, exactly as I did. So I put mine behind my head.

He kept arching his shoulders as though distracted by the view out the kitchen window of the small courtyards, terraces, and brick alleyways.

"Cosmo Giovanni owned that brown Tudor, you know," he said. "He had it built himself out of solid granite. Filled it with seventeen children, including two sets of twins. Ever hear of anything like that? Two sets of twins?"

No one said anything, so he repeated the question. "Did you ever hear of such a thing? Two sets?"

Still, no one spoke.

"That Giovanni," he went on undeterred. "He was a millionaire before he even had his first child. He had a couple of restaurants that were quite popular, but you don't want to know where his money really came from."

He winked at me, and I hoped that meant the end of Giovanni's tale. But soon he was going on about stealing the guy's tomatoes when he was a kid, and then Italian food — *real* Italian food — and I stopped paying attention.

Carey rolled his eyes and looked at the clock. Its ticking filled the kitchen, the vibrations suspending us up and above the room where, for those delayed moments between each stroke of the second hand, I got a kind of unspeakably bizarre, and yet detached view of the four of us sitting there.

I could easily see through my old man's nonsense. Deflecting the truth with incessant chatter had become second nature to him. He wasn't about to let any silences occur without trying to fill them. The last thing he wanted was anyone bringing up the one thing that was on everyone's mind. Not that anyone was about to. And Mark would not have wanted us to, either. He may have come off as aloof and arrogant at 19, but he was a good kid, and would have never intentionally hurt a soul.

Silence...

Mark wasn't a jock but he was definitely one of the cool kids. When he was in high school, he and his "boys" would sometimes hang out on Friday and Saturday nights at my mother's house. He had fixed up one of the attic rooms into a bedroom, and with the extra beds that were up there he created make-shift couches. He also added my parent's old console-stereo from the living room, and a snowy-screened old tube TV that was daisy-chained to the cable downstairs so they could watch WrestleMania and God knows what else.

Most of them were on the wrestling team themselves, but they weren't the usual mainstream athletic-types. These were leather jacket-wearing, motorcycle-riding, shop class-taking dudes who were too cool to engage in much conversation with me, the old man older brother. Yet as overconfident as they were, they were subdued. Aside from listening to music too loud and watching wrestling, who knows what else was going on up there, but I am sure it was nothing more than the probable and occasional sneaking in of some liquor or perhaps a little bit of weed.

I mean, Mark wasn't a stoner by any stretch of the game, nor was he into any other drugs. I would know — trust me. But he was no boy scout. I knew that he "delved" because late one night during the summer before his junior year I got a call from the Hampton Falls Police in New Hampshire that he was in a car that had been pulled over for speeding on the highway. Mark and his friend Danny had taken the 90-or-so minute cruise up to the boardwalk at Hampton Beach in Danny's car. Anyway, the police found remnants of marijuana; I don't even remember what — roaches or a bowl in the ashtray — and they arrested them.

As cool as he may have thought he was at that age, man, the look on his face when he saw me at the police station went right through me: pure terror. I just wanted to make it better for him. I would have taken his part, if I could have. Heck, I had done that and much worse by the time I was his age.

But I had to at least act angry if nothing more than virtual silence on the drive back to Boston. He didn't even deny any of it, or claim that the pot was his friend's. He only wanted to know if I were going to tell our mom, and I said through a stern face, "What?! I have to think about that." But that was bluff, too.

He had to appear in court about a month later and I wound up taking him. And though the case was "continued without a finding," my mother never knew a thing.

3:51 AM

I looked up from the desk and saw Rosie peeking over the partition. She was standing on a chair that she had quietly slid over to the front of the stage.

"Hey," I said.

"You looked so serene there, I didn't want to bug ya."

Serene, ha.

"You know, they have a word for people like you," I said.

"Well, Mr. Julien, I've heard most of the words people have used about me, and I could do without hearing the rest, thank you very much." She hopped down, her head disappearing like a puppet, replaced by one hand with a cigarette poised between two fingers. I was struck by the beauty of her hand at that moment, so graceful, even elegant.

"I'm just going to have me one of these," she said. "Will you join me?"

"I'm right behind you," I said to her hand. "Just give me a minute."

When I got to the alleyway stairs, she was sitting near the top with her small legs crossed at the knees. I stood at the bottom, and silently shook a cigarette loose from my pack. It was flattened a bit, so I pinched it back into shape. I didn't light it until I was sitting beside her.

She was looking straight ahead silently, as though she were alone. There were holes in the threadbare terrycloth robe she had on, and a faint odor of vomit that made me catch my breath.

I watched the match burn down, blowing it out just before it reached my thumb, then waited for it to stop smoking and threw it over my shoulder.

"So your angel found your teeth for you?" I said, finally.

She took a long drag off her unfiltered Camel and held it a few seconds before letting out a steady stream of blue smoke. She raised her head slightly, blowing it up and away from where we sat. Then she looked me as though wondering if I were putting her on.

Everyone else called her crazy, but she wouldn't expect that from me.

Still, she was silent.

"At the very least, you were lucky," I said. "What would you do without your teeth?"

"I would do just fine. I've had to do with a lot less than those teeth, you know," she said sounding irritated. "No one even noticed, anyway."

She smiled, displaying her bare gums. "You've got to be happy with absolutely nothing, before you can truly see the beauty in anything. It's just kissing the hag, is all, Boston Boy."

"Kissing the hag?"

"Or, maybe it's listening to your angel."

"*My* angel?"

"Or your goddess, or call it your bloody third eye for all I care. But it's all the same."

"What does *kissing the hag* mean?"

"Well, according to the Irish myths, the king is he who comes *to know*. And as he passes through his time on the throne," she bent slightly forward and looked straight at me, "which *is* life, the goddess presents herself to him in many forms. She is never greater than he is, but she's capable of giving him more than he is able to comprehend without her."

"You mean gifts? Like helping him win Megabucks

or something?"

"Well, let's just say that if he can accept what she offers, he is set free from all that binds him."

"Set free? How?"

"Well, it has nothing to do with the world around us, I can attest to that, though it has everything to do with what you *see. Your* world, Mr. Julien."

She curled her top lip as if in disgust and I thought she'd caught the smell of puke from her slippers, but continued speaking: "She is made hideous by the eyes that refuse to see true beauty — the eyes of arrogance and cruelty," she said slowly, her snarl growing more pronounced with every word.

"So, how can you tell if she's a goddess *or* an angel? I mean, if she's so ugly?"

"The true king is he who meets her with kindness." She nodded her head and spoke more deliberately. "In the eyes of grace she is redeemed. Then she *and* the redeemer are released. Have you ever heard the tale of the hag by the well?"

"I'm not sure," I said. "Probably not."

"It's about the five sons of the Irish King, and how they set out one day hunting and found themselves lost. Thirsty and exhausted, they set off one by one in search of water.

"Fergus was the first to go, and he soon came upon a well. Beside the round stone wall stood an old woman keeping guard. Her skin was black as soot from filth, her coarse hair a wiry-gray mass." Raising her hands above her head, Rosie twisted her fingers into arthritic claws.

"The old woman's plump, freckled and peeling belly was exposed," she said, wrapping her arms around her own bloated midsection. "Her legs were warped, as though they'd been crushed beneath the wheels of a wagon. She had one green tooth that curved out of her mouth like a tusk and almost touched her ear, and her nostrils looked like a pig's..." Rosie snorted a couple of times for emphasis "...only running in a constant current and crusted around the edges, greener than the sickle protruding from her mouth."

"O.K.," I said, and held up my hand. "I've got the visual."

She took a quick look at me sideways, smirked, and went on:

"'Do you guard this well?' Fergus said, looking away in disgust.

"'I do,' said the hag.

"'Would you allow me to take away some water, then?' he asked.

"'Certainly,' said she. 'All that I ask in return is that you bestow a single kiss upon my cheek.'

Rosie stopped and looked directly at me. "And what do you think was his response?"

"Um, he closed his eyes, held his breath, and puckered up?"

"'I'd rather die from thirst than give *you* a kiss,' he told her, and rode off. When he returned he told his brothers that he had found no water."

"So the next brother goes out to look, right?"

"Yes, indeed. And the next, and the next. All three encounter the same old woman beside the very same old well. All three refuse to kiss her."

"That leaves the fifth brother," I said, assuredly, hoping that she noted I was paying attention.

"Yes, the fifth brother. His name was Niall. By the time he met the old woman at the well, his thirst was terribly great, and as soon as he saw her, he cried, 'Let me have some water, woman!'

"'I will give it freely,' she said, 'if you would bestow a single kiss upon my cheek.'

"Niall smiled at the old crone and jumped down from his horse. 'Not only will I kiss you, dear woman, but I'll hug you as well,' he said. Then he bent over and placed his arms around her crooked frame, and kissed her softly on her filthy cheek.

"And when he stood back, he held in his arms the most beautiful woman he'd ever laid eyes upon. A long and graceful body had she: straight and queenly limbs, flesh of the most gorgeous golden hue, and eyes the deep indigo of the full moon's midnight sky. Her scarlet hair was spun from the blazing sunset itself, and her teeth glowed like the mother of everything pearl."

"And she rode off with him into sunset," I said, "and the two lived happily ever after in his castle on the hill."

"Miss *Rosie* will tell the story, if Mr. Julien *doesn't* mind.

"He does not."

"'Who are you?' exclaimed Niall," Rosie said, throwing her hands up into the darkness around us.

"'I am Royal Rule,' said the goddess."

"'But I am Niall, Ruler of Tara. *I am Royal Rule.'*

"'At first you saw me as ugly and loathsome,' she said, 'and in the end, beautiful — such is Royal Rule. For the truest battles are won not with force or conflict, but with gentleness of heart. Go now. Take this water to your brothers. From this day forward, all the kingdom — spreading far beyond the province of Tara— and the supreme power shall be yours and your children's.'"

I waited a moment. "So you must be able to see the beauty within the ugliness, before you can truly appreciate it?" I said.

"Before you can truly *possess* it. You must be happy with nothing, before you can be happy with everything."

I had no response. After a few moments I threw my cigarette on the stair beneath me and crushed it under my heel.

She pushed on my leg hard with her hand, then patted out her own cigarette very carefully on the wooden stair beside her and stashed what was left in the pocket of her robe for later.

"Go on then," she said. "And don't get lost in your own thoughts again."

"How do you know when your angel is speaking to you?" I asked, and blew at the specks of gray ash beside my shoe.

She took a breath to answer, but I wasn't finished, "You told me once that angels show things to you. Do they ever come in dreams? And how do you know that it isn't in fact some demon?"

"Slow down," she said, but I couldn't stop myself.

"I mean, if you hear angels, can you hear the devils too? And how can you tell the difference?"

"First things first," she said. She pulled a pale yellow kerchief from the pocket of her robe, and she held the washed out material in her teeth as she quickly gathered her thick, uneven crop of chestnut hair with both hands. Then she tied it with the kerchief somewhere in the back. I noticed how the dark strands were only flecked lightly with steely strands of gray. It seemed a testament to her strength, her resilience.

"Whenever I hear my angel I can tell it's her because it is the sweetest sound," she said.

"But what *kind* of a sound? How do you know?"

"I know," she said thoughtfully, "because it is always the truth." Then, with a certain authority, "Because whatever *she* says cannot be questioned."

"How do you know it's a girl?"

"Well, they aren't actually girls or boys; they don't have any bodies. I always have this impression of a little girl whenever she's near," she said, smiling again, but shyly this time and hiding her face for a moment with the collar of her robe.

"How do you know it's the truth?"

"I know it's the truth because it is quite often something for which I didn't even know to look. It goes past my own understanding, you see? Something that's revealed to me at the very moment I most need it. I just know. Like an answer, but one that comes to you from a place you know exists only because you feel it." Then quickly at me, beaming with pride, "Like ... *a thought*," she said. "Do you know the difference between seeking knowledge, and then searching for answers for which only you would have any use?"

"Well, sure, I guess," I said. "You mean, like soul-searching? I've done my share."

"Of course you have," she said, "or you wouldn't be sitting here now."

I'd felt for a moment I was beginning to grasp what she was saying, but that last statement seemed to require more thought than I could give it.

Me — here?

She pushed my leg again, harder than before, and said, "When you go searching for the truth and find it, don't you ever question where it came from? You wouldn't be giving yourself any credit for it, would you now?"

"Well... I don't know," I said.

"Always remember what happened to the man who went through life acting as if he'd less to learn than everyone else."

"What was that?"

"In the end he learned a lot less, didn't he?"

"He learned less," I said slowly. "And I know what you mean, regarding those angel voices that is, or impressions or what ever anyone calls it, but I call it the truth, too," and fumbled a bit. "And I attribute the revelation to... grace, maybe. What else?"

Her hands were open in front of her, but directed at me, "Your angel," she said in a whisper. "That is your angel speaking to you, Mr. Julien."

I thought of my life, from that point in the ICU bed until now. I considered all that I'd learned, and gained, and grown into, over that time. When I tried to connect it to this past year, it didn't fit. It was another life entirely. None of what I'd learned then was applicable now. It was all rendered null and void the morning I found Mark.

"What is a lifetime worth if it is to end this way?" I said.

I had a vague sense of someone else listening, and thought of the audience: *I must be coherent for them.* I tried to think of one poignant question, one that would induce an eloquent, articulate response and sum it all up for them.

"Of what value are lessons learned and truths revealed, if it is all to be swept away to nothingness? I mean, who cares from where it came, if everywhere you go, you're filled with fear. I think I'm even afraid to sleep." I wanted to say more but I didn't have the words, as though I had forgotten my lines.

"Why shouldn't certain things give you a fright?" she said. "Some of your worst nightmares have come true, haven't they?"

A lens turned in my head, and I saw what she meant in perfect clarity. I was stunned at the sense and simplicity of it. I put my hand to my collar bone remembering how real Mark's small cheek felt as it lay against my shoulder in the dream earlier that night.

"Do angels come to you in dreams? Do they appear as themselves? Do demons do the same?"

"Here, here now. Who's been having bad dreams, then?"

"I keep dreaming about my brother, and they are always the same. In all of them he is small, maybe three or four. They didn't distress me at all, though, not until today."

She was silent, and nodded for me to continue.

"I took a nap before work," I said, and lit another cigarette. "I wasn't having the best day, or the easiest time falling asleep. Anyway, this dream went along as fast and choppy as most, you know, where everyone zips around as if in a sixteen-millimeter home movie.

"I was in my mother's kitchen, blowing out candles on a cake. It was some kind of celebration for me, but I didn't know for what. I knew it wasn't my birthday. The next thing I know I'm down the hallway in the living room, and my mother and Carey are holding themselves and crying hysterically.

"'Mark's dead, he's dead,' they keep saying over and over. I look down to the bottom drawer of the family desk: The same cherry Queen Anne, standing beneath the same Wyeth print since time began for me. The drawer is open wide and there's toddler-Mark, lying inside. The tiny features of his face are all the same light blue, but softly luminous, like the sky or a robin's egg."

So different from dead-Mark, hanging from his bed sheet: swollen and purple; the bruised, hideous caricature of his 19-year-old face.

Rosie sat quite still, not smiling at all now, but listening closely.

"I turned calmly to Carey and my mother and, putting my hands on both of their backs, I reassuringly told them to leave the room and that I was going to take care of everything. Then I bent over and picked Mark up from the drawer and held him to my shoulder, as if I knew just what needed to be done. The full weight of his body was so real, so intensely familiar; the smooth, warm sensation of his cheek as his head lay flat against my collar bone. It was as if he'd just fallen asleep on a car ride home, or on the couch watching cartoons an hour ago." I paused and took a drag of my cigarette.

Rosie drew the stub of the half-smoked Camel from her pocket and squeezed the sides lightly to bring it back to shape, then lightly packed it a few times on her knee. I lit a match and cupped it with both hands for her, even though the air was quite still.

"Mmm…" She said and puffed on the flame. "So he

wasn't dead, then?"

"Oh, he was quite dead," I said. "I knew he was dead, but I wasn't upset at all. I just walked him around the room and rubbed his back in slow circular motions, whispering, 'Just breathe, Mark, just breathe.' In a few seconds I felt his chest rise against mine and his eyes darted open, and then blinked. It was just as if I had startled him out of a nap, but his eyes were full of trust, like when he was a very small and he'd look up at me from his carriage. That was it.

"But I awoke in a panic and kept looking at my clock and saying out loud over and over 'Eight-fifty, eight-fifty, eight-fifty...' But that made no sense. Slowly I realized it was a dream and that I was now awake, and then I just lay there for a long time. I couldn't get that picture of his tiny face all blue, and those warm, trusting eyes, out of my head. I still can't."

She put her hand on my thigh and kept it there this time. I thought she was going to say something, but she didn't.

"If angels come to you in your dreams, can devils as well? I always thought I had something to learn from my dreams, but..."

"Now calm yourself, Mr. Julien. Devils *do* throw their voices in attempts to try and confuse the likes of you, and me — those who *search*."

I felt oddly proud for a moment that she would include me in her category.

"But I wouldn't be telling the truth if I said any demon would have a chance with you."

"What do you mean?"

"I mean that they can't take what's not theirs. They already have all the liars and haters. They only torment those who look, and suffer, and *bleed*."

She said 'bleed' very slowly, and tilted her head my way. I looked down at my feet, and held my wrist, running my thumb up and down the inside, over the lattice-work of scars.

She knew about Mark, but what else did she know?

"No," she said. "They can only throw their voices and try to make you lose your way."

"But how can you tell the difference, if you listen to anything in the first place?"

"The truth is always the hardest to hear. So, you must always choose what's most difficult. The easy way out is always wrong. It doesn't take much effort to be evil, though it may seem otherwise at times." She grabbed some of her robe and tugged lightly for a second, as if she just remembered something important.

"Besides," she went on, "angels can't speak anything but the truth. All the devil *can* do is lie."

I cupped my face in both hands and let out an abysmal sigh. "But how do you *know*, especially if it's not a choice? You don't choose your dreams."

"You have to listen to what it *tells* you. Anyway, angels, or devils for that matter, don't come to you in your dreams," she said. "But those who have gone before us sometimes do, especially soon after they go. And they always have a message."

"But what the hell could my brother be trying to tell me with a nightmare? Keep up the torment? The worst is yet to come?"

"No, no, no," she said. "What might it be that you need to know?"

I covered my face in my hands again, straining for an answer. "I haven't a fricken' clue."

"You don't see? He's telling you he knows quite well that you would have helped him if you'd had the chance. He's saying he knows that you could have, and quite easily, too."

I was at a complete loss.

"And you know why it all matters. You just forgot for a little while, that's all. You're only human. It matters, and I will tell you this for certain because I know it to be true, because once someone occupies a place in your heart, they remain there forever. They become a part of you as much as your legs, or your arms, or your fingers."

Silence...

I felt like I really knew Rosie sometimes, and had to remind myself that the details I actually did know of her life were scant and few, though they always have, and still do, paint a vivid image for me...

She said one night, "I had a house once. Well, it was the ground floor apartment, but the whole floor to us, and with so many rooms I couldn't count them all — and a garden out back. I had just started to grow tomatoes when everything began to go..." Her voice lagged off a bit and I knew I probably shouldn't ask, even though I wanted to know what everything was, and where it went.

On another occasion she told me that she went to the parish school in the village where she grew up.

"Oh, it was only one room in a small stone frame with a fireplace in the corner. If your parents could pay an extra few shillings you got to sit by the fire in the winter and upfront by the teacher during the rest of the year. My father was a foreman at the mill and a hard worker and could spare the extra shillings. But he had a mean streak, especially if he'd been hitting the whisky. And he'd fork the coins over only on the really cold days in the dead of winter; we never could sit up in the front.

"But I loved school. I loved reading and writing and learning about other places. I stayed on until the eighth and final year, when I was sixteen, and a young nun came in to teach us. Sister Bridgette Delaney, from Dublin, and a wee pip of a thing. Didn't look much older than me, and she certainly caused a stir when she first arrived, riding around on a bike in her habit, and stopping to talk with men gathered outside the pub for a smoke.

"Sister Bridgette had brought quite a little library that she'd kept in a large bookcase behind her desk: from Shakespeare and Shelly, to Virginia Woolf and George Orwell. She took a real shine to me and would let me borrow a volume whenever I liked, though only one at a time. I had read through almost her entire collection, reading each book completely and returning it, before she'd let me borrow another. Then, suddenly, her and the book case were gone. Apparently the bishop came for a visit and while driving through town he spied her sitting on the hood of a car, eating an ice cream cone, all while chatting up a football team who had only just finished practicing, a few of the boys in my school.

"But she gave me a love for stories that I'll never forget. She showed me that, even though made up, they're also about so much that's true. Do you know what I mean? Did you know that I wanted to be a teacher when I came here to the States?"

I never would have imagined that.

"But my Jimmy, he had his eyes set on being a musician. He could play that piano, you know. And he was really good. His grandfather taught him all the old ballads but it was the ragtime and blues numbers that really caught his fancy and before long he was teaching himself the songs. He had dreams of playing in the great jazz clubs of New York and New Orleans. Oh, he listened to the greatest of them, every night on the radio, and had a stack of records higher than my nose. But it was no sooner after we got here and he started practicing with some of the blokes — musicians and the like at the club where he was waitering — that he tasted the needle and that was it. Wasn't long before we had nothing, of course. And then he had the accident with our baby..." her head dropped just then as though in shame, or something deeper, and she slowly shook it a few times.

"But I really don't want to talk about that. I never do. I was going to be a teacher, though. I think I would've made a right good one, too."

4:23 AM

"There's only one other time I felt so…" Then I stopped. "Never mind. It doesn't matter."

Rosie was not so easily dissuaded. "*Everything matters*," she said, and put her fingers lightly to her chin, thoughtfully stroking. "There was only one time you felt sooo…?"

"Disconnected," I said.

"Oh, really now? And when would that have been?"

"Well, about five years ago — in London," I said, knowing now there was no turning back. I didn't really want to tell this story because I never had, but I couldn't bring myself to offend Rosie by cutting her off.

"Remember I told you about the time I'd lived over there? As an exchange student?"

"I remember," she said, still in that same posture of intent interest. "Didn't you have employment at a restaurant, then?"

"Yes, my visa was good for a year, and I'd signed up for only one semester at a college north of the city. So, when that finished I moved to London and got a job waiting tables at an American place in Covent Garden."

"Oh, right. So what happened there?"

"I wasn't at work when it happened. I was at home, in my flat in Brixton."

"And?"

"Well, I had been out all night after work: clubbing until the early morning hours, and then hit China Town after that. I got home just before dawn and crashed hard, but lay drifting, half asleep, until I bolted fully awake just after daybreak, and... I don't know." I put my hands on my head, pressing my fngers into my scalp and massaging, struggling for precise words.

"It was as if all the definition and structure of my life had been swept away; the framework around me simply dismantled while I slept. The last thing I remembered was envisioning the days that lay before me — like pages on a calendar being ripped and tossed to the wind, and whatever meaning they may have had fading from sight. All this in a matter of seconds.

"The only sensation that comes close to was how, as a child at St. Augustine's grade school, the nuns would continuously say that God "always was", and I'd contemplate the concept of Him having no beginning. That notion mystified me so much I'd get completely lost in it and, sometimes for an instant, it was almost like stepping off a ledge into this vast incomprehensible space. *That* rush is the only feeling I can equate with what I felt that morning in Brixton: the sensation of plunging into an immense pool, and the overwhelming movement above and beneath and beside me, like tides rising and falling all at the same time. Then, nothing."

"Nothing?" she said.

"Just a deafening silence, louder than words — a horrifying nothingness."

"Well, what did you do then?"

"I jumped out of my bed and ran about the room in a complete panic. I didn't know what to do. It was like I had amnesia. Nothing meant anything; all meaning had been taken from me. I said the *Our Father* over and over. It just came to me. And even harder to explain but, at that moment, I didn't even know what prayer meant, and I kept getting lost in it, forgetting how it went. So 'I just kept starting it again and again."

After a long pause, I continued. "Then, slowly, as I

paced around the room, the morning came back into focus, but not right away. Not completely, anyway. After a few minutes I knew that it was Sunday morning, and that I was in Brixton. But I was still scared, and maybe even a bit in shock — I don't quite know.

"But I was gripped with the overwhelming urge to call someone, and I reached for the receiver and dialed up my friend Vicky, in Windsor. As I listened to the ringing through the receiver, I was overcome with the fear that she wouldn't be there. Not just absent, but not existing."

"And did she?" Rosie said.

"Did she what?"

"Did she answer the call? Your friend Vicky. Did she pick up the phone?"

"Oh yeah... yes. I woke her up, and she wasn't pleased. It was only about six a.m., and on a Sunday."

"So what did that tell you?"

"Well, not much. But it made me feel secure, in a peculiar way, to know that everything *was* still there. But the oddest thing happened in the launderette, a bit later."

"Oh, we're in the laundry now, are we?"

"Well, yes. I hung up the phone and tried to sleep more, but couldn't. So, after a few hours I decided to get up and do some laundry."

"Aren't we the domestic one?" she said and nudged me with her elbow.

"Not really. But I was still pretty shaken, and basically just went over there to give myself something to do. But the oddest thing happened.

"Brixton was a predominantly black neighborhood, which just a few years before had been home to a few race riots and car bombings. Though I never saw any real conflict, people pretty much kept to themselves — blacks and whites that is, separate — and then there were smaller pockets of Pakistanis and Indians, etc. The area was pretty diverse, but everyone just kept to their own. Maybe that's just a foreigner's view. I don't know."

"Well, at any rate it sounds like a rough place — riots and bombings?"

"Those things happened years before I showed up."

"Well, why ever did you move into such a place?"

"I took a bus from school to London, bought a newspaper, and circled the cheapest flat I could find. I didn't think about it, really. Besides, I never had a lick of trouble in the time I lived there, and I would come home at all hours, but that's not the point."

"Well, Mr. Julien, sir, what is the point, pray tell?"

"I'm not really sure. But I'm kind of getting to it. You see, I had this encounter with a black girl in the launderette."

"Oh even though you were so distraught you had time to chat up some sweet, young thing?"

"It wasn't like that, Rosie. First of all, I didn't 'chat her up.' Secondly, she was only about seven or eight years old. And the whole interaction took only about three seconds. It was really quite simple. I'd dropped a sock on the other side of the washer I was loading, and she jumped up from her seat and handed it to me."

"That's it?"

"Not quite. I was still pretty shaken up from that spell, or dream, or whatever it was. I mean, I had no clue what it meant, and I was still a bit frightened, and kind of insecure. Anyway, I looked down from stuffing my clothes in the machine, and there she was, standing with an outstretched hand, and the most beautiful smile I'd ever seen."

"Every smile is beautiful," she said, then thought about it for a few seconds. "Well, most are, anyway."

"This wasn't every smile," I said, "But somehow I knew it was *mine*."

"Yours?"

"It was *for* me, and came from somewhere — I'm not sure where — but beyond her little face. And it was like, I don't know, one of the sweetest luxuries of my life, but one that I kept... forgetting?" I struggled for words. I hoped that Rosie would chime in and give me a hand but she had unequivocally given me the floor.

"All I can say is that it comforted me in a way only what is dearest to you can," I said. "It's so hard to articulate, but I could *see* everything in the moments following: How it could be — should be — the connection. How everyone and everything is joined in a certain order, but constant too. And how we all belong to, or rather, are responsible for one another. Because nothing we do, or say, or even feel, happens without effects elsewhere. Do you understand?"

"I think I do, a little bit," she said. "And what happened then?"

"What happened? I don't really know, but I was released from 'something so big, so awful, it transcended even my mental vocabulary. I'd gotten up in such a panic, in absolute horror, almost as if I just realized that I'd killed someone, without knowing I had, or by mistake... I guess, now, looking back, it had something to do with everything."

"What's *everything*?" Her tone sounded more like an inquest.

"Everything I'd been through when I was so unhappy, when I was so screwed up, but never *truly* experienced because I was so ... screwed up." I felt odd just then, referring to my own alcoholism.

"So... shut down." I said.

I thought of the night that landed me in the ICU. Had I ever imagined anything worse than lying on a mattress saturated with my own blood, three heart beats away from my own grave?

"It's all relative, you know?" I said. "The ICU, my brother's noose..."

"What are you going on about?" she said.

"It doesn't matter," I said. "But back to the launderette and the little girl. After her smile, all that fear and trepidation was swept away. Gone."

"Like the pages on the calendar?"

"Yeah," I said, slowly, surprised at the connection *she* drew. "I suppose so. But all that I valued in this world, this existence, was apparent to me, and everything was in-place. I was all at once enveloped by the day and my life, and the simple, supreme joy in, I don't know… having laundry to do."

"And what did this all come to mean? What did it *tell* you?"

"I thought that episode, when I awoke in my little London flat, was the lowest I'd ever go. As far as I *could* go, onto the furthest slope I'd ever been. And though I knew I might be thrust there again sometime, I'd never go any further. And I also knew that I could take it, even without any concrete definition of what it all specifically meant. I knew it was very real, and somehow, very important, something that might aid me in the future."

"Like armor… for a future battle perhaps?" she asked, but as if she were also giving me the answer.

"Armor? I never looked at it that way, but I suppose you could. I guess I saw it more… I'm' not quite sure… Indicative?"

"Indicating what, then?"

"The furthest I'd ever go."

"From your *home*?" she said, and this time I knew it was a test.

"No," I said. "Spiritually—emotionally… It was the deepest I would ever reach. And that frightened me. I knew I'd return there. It was as if someone were telling me my own story."

"But you said you hadn't a clue as to what it meant."

"I didn't know *what* it was. But I knew it had meaning. Silence louder than sound. Emptiness. Everything was gone, Rosie. It was my worst possible nightmare. And you're right: worst nightmares do come true. It felt prophetic, like a warning. Do you see what I mean?

"I do," she said. "But do you?"

"What do you mean?"

"You said that was the only other time you felt so disconnected, yes?"

"That I can recall, other than earlier today, when I woke from that nightmare about my brother. But it wasn't the same."

"Well, did you not tell me of another time when you paced around a room in a panic, repeating the same words over and over?"

Silence...

I looked up from the stairs where we sat into the darkness and saw the silhouette of my brother's twisted body as it hung from the beam in my mother's attic.

I didn't kill him, I didn't kill him I didn't kill him, I just kept saying as I paced under him... *I didn't kill him, I didn't kill him...*

Silence...

4:49 AM

Andrea Alvarez appeared at the bottom of the stairs. Rosie and I both looked at her. Andrea's slender, almost six-foot frame was dressed in a plaid skirt, blouse, and red knitted vest which, I'm quite sure, was chosen from the backstage walk-in closet to accentuate the ruby lines of her kilt. She was the quintessential donation-bin fashion plate. I loved the assonance of her first and last names together and always used both when addressing her.

"Hey, Andrea Alvarez. Where are you off to? Bagpipe practice?"

Rosie whacked my side with the backside of her hand.

"What the Christ do you think you and our organization are doing?" Andrea Alvarez crossed her arms and grabbed her shoulders. "I'm freezing to death!"

"I'm sorry," I lowered my voice, "but the heat is all the way up. You can have another blanket."

"No, no. It's too late now. Just let me into the ladies room please before Reverend Kyle sets off another mice bomb, please. This entire building is built over cancer, you know."

"I know," I said, and stood to make my way for the stage and the key. It was tied to a foot long piece of wood with a capital L drawn quite carefully on both sides with a black felt pen. It was always to be returned to the very same hook on the wall behind the desk.

She followed closely behind me. "You most certainly do know," she said. "Mice bombs. And you're all in on it. I saw you planting one at Dunkin' Donuts on Tremont. You didn't know I saw you, but I did."

"Sorry about that," I said, and handed her the key.

Andrea was in her mid-sixties with long black hair and carried herself like a model. Drugs and insanity washed away the edges of her striking features, leaving only the remnants of a distant, vanished beauty. She was once a stewardess, so she said, and sometimes I watched her walk up the corridor between the partitions, imagining it as an aisle between the seats on an airplane, where *she* once handed out pillows and blankets.

I grabbed the clipboard, took the long way around the dorms and walked through the men's cots on my way back to the stairs, doing a quick rounds check, all the while hoping that Rosie would still be there.

I sat down beside her in silence and flipped through the list quickly now that I was in some light. All clear and copasetic, check, check, check.

After a few moments I looked over and Rosie's hands were spread out before her. The palms facing forward and she carefully examined the backs.

"Now who's lost in *her* own thoughts," I said.

"I had a daughter, once," she said. "She died when she was very small, still a little girl. This was way back, not long after I came over here."

"You mentioned that once, and said there was an accident." I did not want her to think I was prying or waiting for an elaboration, so I just said, "That's awful... truly awful," and looked back to the list, though I was really done with it for now.

She put her hands slowly down to her lap where they rested perfectly still. Her face radiated for a few seconds and then faded before she continued.

"You know, sometimes I can't sleep, and I lie awake in bed or outside on some bench, and my mind wanders back to the old days. Sometimes I don't want it to, but I just can't stop it. And you know, I can't remember how some songs go, though I'm sure at one time they were my favorites. And I see faces of those I was quite fond of at one time, but their names escape me. When I try to remember, it is all too fast and fleeting, like trying to look into the windows of a speeding train..." Her voice got a bit raspy, and trailed off for a moment, only to come back full force:

"But do you know what? The image of my girl's small hands is so clear to me; the fine blond hairs on the back of her tiny knuckles, and the little dimples that appeared just below when she'd open them up wide."

I almost looked away, sure Rosie was about to cry. Then she unfolded her hands out in front of her again, inspecting them.

"I used to press down on them as if they were little buttons or bells." She laughed breathlessly and shook her head.

"I almost wish it wasn't so close, but do you know what I realize then? I know she *is* that close. Only now she is before me, and not peering out of my past.

"And then, I wonder if those songs I can't remember are actually ones I haven't heard yet, or these hurling faces are simply ones I've yet to meet. They are just sweet harmonies and warm hearts prepared for me, waiting for me still, somewhere."

She stopped again and faced me. "Then I'm filled with a comfort that carries me through all of these days and nights, Mr. Julien, and I say to my angel: Take all of this to *Him*. Take all of my pain and dirt. Turn it all into prayers for those who are far from Him. Or for anyone who has less than me."

Her gaze dropped off to the side. Without warning, I found myself seeing her as pitiful. Pitiful and drunk. This time I was sure she was on the verge of tears by the pronounced curl of her lips, even without her teeth.

Who has less than Rosie?

"I look around me here at the mission," she went on,

"and around the city. I watch men and women pass by, dressed in the finest clothes... and me in rags. I wonder if I asked them to describe the hands they held the night before, or the ones they kissed goodbye that morning, if they could do so in as much detail as I see my girl's. Do they understand with as much delight... where it comes from?

"And there are other times when I lie there at night, and I'm stone-sober, and the pieces of songs that I can't remember don't go away, and the only comfort I have in the world is how my baby girl's fingers felt against my cheek; it's all I can think of. That, and maybe my next drink, or sometimes why my Jimmy treated me the way he did in the end."

"I don't ever wonder how it all went the way it did..." her voice trailed off, distant and small, only to return full force with: "I was there," she said. "Thank you very much."

"But sometimes I do think: Why? Why did *I* have to? Then I remember what truly keeps me going, but that's a secret."

"A secret?" I said, "I didn't think you and I had any."

"Cause it's about sacrifice, probably the highest form of prayer," she said. "Oh, that and compassion, I suppose."

She shook her head as if to erase the distraction and caught my eyes, looking into them deeply. "But you know that," she said.

There she goes again. "I do?"

"Problem is, it loses its power if you talk about it. You just have to accept what you've got, or had once... and be grateful." She stopped, and then said in a low chuckle, "Grateful that you can shut it all off with a bottle, or a lovely dream of a small hand."

On impulse, I leaned over and softly kissed her cheek.

"Do you realize what you just did?" she said, her one eye opening wide in surprise.

"Yes," I said through a strained whisper, though, at

the time, I was without a clue.

"But I think you already have done this before," she said, "and forgot that as well."

"Forgot what?"

"Kissing the hag," she said.

Silence...

I keep a picture of Mark on my dresser. He's about three or four and is lying sideways in the green wingback chair in the living room, sound asleep. I look at the faded Polaroid, and his braided yellow sweater, the turtleneck jersey and corduroy overalls. I remember picking the clothes out that morning when I dressed him.

My parents were away for the day at the wedding of a relative somewhere out in the Berkshires. A bright and sunny Sunday, sometime in early September, and Mark and I had been to the park all morning. Then, in the afternoon, we went to a carnival at Saint Augustine's School, which was just at the end of our block. We ate hot dogs, drank orange soda, and had his face painted like a clown.

I loved to take him places where I was known. It was a gas to run into old teachers of mine, as they'd see me with him and shake their heads, and say something like: "Oh, no, not another one." He was a smaller version of me, with the same curly brown hair, the same blue eyes. Being seen with him was close to the way something you do exceptionally well makes you feel, but without having to lift a finger.

Nowadays, when I see that picture just before leaving my room, in a flash I breathe in the aroma of dry leaves and sticks that permeated the crisp autumn air that afternoon and I am filled with a sense of how exquisitely perfect a single day can be. How everything can be simple and splendid at the same time, just by being where it was all supposed to be.

But, for a long time after Mark died, I would find myself standing in front of my dresser, coaching myself when my gaze fell upon the photograph: "You must go, and live, and strive to be happy. Just reserve a place for this. Someday, the memory will be sweet again."

Not that I believed it at the time. I had no real sense of the person I was, or the brother I'd been, and was unable to see how anything could possibly be as perfect as I thought that day had been. Not with part of me missing, the part that was me *and* Mark. And gone with it was a degree of innocence I hadn't even known was there until it had to be replaced by the realization that sometimes there are no second chances. And we don't have all that much time to figure this out.

"You should have left it better with me, kiddo," I'd say to the picture before I left the room now. "You just should have left it better."

5:10 AM

There was a loud crack of sorts from the women's side, and I heard a somewhat muted commotion coming from the bathroom so I sprang from my feet, leaving Rosie on the stairs.

"For Chris' sakes" slurred some indignant female guest as I hurried past her bed.

"You are not supposed to be in here!" I heard Andrea saying.

"Oh, screw you! You think you are the bathroom monitor, or something?"

Andrea Alvarez stood just inside the Ladies' room door, holding tightly to the inside handle, not allowing an older woman, Alice, to enter.

"Reverend Kyle says one-at-a-time," She was telling Alice. "Besides, you people want to start fires in here, I know. I have seen it many times."

"Hey, quiet down, please. People are trying to sleep. You can let her in if you are all finished," I told her.

"That's not the imperative," she said indignantly.

Imperative. Please! "Yeah, well I make the rules when I am here. And if you want to get technical, I shouldn't even let you have the key. I should be opening the door for you."

"That's the goddam problem with this government. Too many bosses. Too many laws that change with every administration."

"Well, my procedures always stay the same. But if you want me to treat you like children, then fine. Just let me know."

I took the key from Andrea, and held it out to Alice, "Do you think you can handle it?"

She grabbed it by the stick-end and headed into the bathroom mumbling something.

"The CIA knows about this already!" Andrea said angrily as she walked away.

"And they should," I said. "And they should."

Back at the stairs another resident had joined Rosie. Joey, also known as Joelle, was not a full-blown transvestite but blurred the lines with his own variety of androgyny by dressing in men's clothes, but accessorizing as a woman with bracelets and rings and broaches, and a women's purse. He was the sweetest guy in the shelter and never gave anyone a lick of trouble. I loved the way he wore a ring on every finger and flashed them in front of your face whenever possible; and the pile of bangles on his wrists and how he would move his arms dramatically as he spoke so that they jangled and clicked together. He was constantly arranging them as if to quiet them down, but it was too apparent that he enjoyed the whole show.

"Have you settled them down, finally? A girl needs her sleep," he said and crushed his cigarette out on the cement floor. His small purse that looked like it was plastic and perhaps made for a child sat neatly on top of his knees; he dropped his lighter in and snapped the top closed with a flourish, and sighed dramatically.

"And by 'girl' I am speaking for the both of us." He said, swinging one arm around Rosie and giving her a half-hug. Then he got up and glided back over to the men's dorm.

I sat down again. Rosie gave my leg another gentle squeeze, and said, "I'll be off to bed, then," before standing on the stair beside me.

"Yeah, and I got to be getting back to the stage," I

said, though I didn't move.

"All the world is a stage, my boy. We are all — every one of us — merely players," she said making her way down the few stairs in measured steps, trying to keep her balance.

"And she quotes Shakespeare, to boot," I said.

She waved an arm forward as if to brush me off, though her back was to me as she walked away.

No sooner had her small frame disappeared into the shadows when there was a heavy rap on the alley door. I rose quickly, but before I got to the top stair there was another strong pounding, quicker this time. Among the rustle of cots, and some half-conscious protests, I looked through the peep hole at the convex frame of a police officer.

"What now?" Kicking the dead-bolt over and flipping through my keys, I shoved the door open.

Stanley Leftwicz — all six feet seven inches of him — stood behind one of the cops who'd been there earlier. Stanley loomed over the guy, erect and stiff, with his shoulders back as if awaiting military inspection.

The policeman lifted his hat a bit and wiped some rain from his brow. "This one's been babbling and screaming like a lunatic all night. He's been driving all the other drunks in the tank crazy."

I looked at the cop, then back at Stanley. He'd never pulled any of that shit before. I mean, Stanley was a drunk, but he wasn't mentally ill.

Great, Mr. Officer. We certainly are your friendly neighborhood toilet. Just knock and flush.

"He'll be fine," I said, and nodded to Stanley, who said, "Yes sir," like an obedient soldier. He went past me into the stairwell where he stood at attention again, awaiting his next command.

Yes sir. Some ex-cons killed me the way they responded as if everything was an order. I knew it was conditioned into the ones who'd done hard time, and had nothing to do with respect, but I was always taken aback by their demeanor, such a sharp contrast to the usual confrontations.

The cop was already back at the cruiser when I slammed the door shut. Turning to Stanley I said, "Do you want a cigarette before you crash?"

"Mmm," he said in agreement.

He remained motionless. I reached into my pocket, pulled out my pack and held open the box. He grabbed at them a few times before clutching one between twitching fingers.

"All right," I said, lighting a match and holding it up for him. "You wait here and I'll go throw some sheets on a bed." I didn't want to stand there with him while he smoked.

Stanley made me uneasy, and it wasn't that I didn't like him. I did. It's just that he's the only person I ever knew who had murdered someone. Manslaughter was the actual charge. He did twelve years for it. I didn't know the details, and I didn't particularly want to. Like I said, I liked him, and I was afraid of letting the brutal facts affect that. I wanted to ignore them, the way you overlook flaws in a friend.

He always gave me a "Hey," when I ran into him, though he never broke that granite expression. His violent past and present indigence notwithstanding, I felt a kind of reverence for him. His facial features seemed cut from a reddish, rough rock; but his complexion glowed beneath a smattering of dirt and scars that I didn't readily see as such. To me, that ruddiness was like a fierce blaze that came from deep within him — the sheer force of survival. And I was in awe of that intensity, though I'd never even contemplated getting close to it.

When I came back to the stairs, he'd finished the cigarette and was standing in exactly the same position.

"Bed's all set," I said. "Your usual one by the laundry room door was free."

"Thank you, sir," he said, and fell out.

"Thank you sir," I said in a whisper to his back. "May I have another?" and it was so strange to me at that moment. I was kidding with myself, but serious. Times like this at the shelter I was momentarily taken aback. It all seemed surreal. Bizarre, in a way that images jump out at you.

Silence…

How strange it felt to see the sunrise the morning of Mark's funeral, since I resented it so intensely. I sat alone in my kitchen in Cambridge, my roommates still asleep, and watched the sky and clouds slowly brighten over the driveway. But the shades of blue and melon and pink had no brilliance at all. They reminded me of bruises—big, multicolored contusions. I don't ever recall any other dawn causing me pain, but this one was brutal, each increase of brightness seeming to reveal an ever-deepening wound.

And then there was the image of one brother at the head of the cortege carrying the coffin of another, to and from the hearse. The sheer oddness of that sight will never leave me. Standing on the sidewalk with one arm protectively over my mother's shoulders, I watched them go up and over the stone stairs of the church, memories of the three of us when Mark was small came in floods: Me watching both of them in the water at the beach, a Fourth of July fireworks display with Mark on my shoulders, the summer the tall Ships first came to Boston, down the end of our street at the park with Mark's carriage always in tow. I was very bossy about the way Carey pushed too fast, and thought he couldn't see as well as I from behind the wide canvass hood of the stroller. And he didn't look where he was going and liked to take corners on two wheels because it made Mark laugh.

"You be very careful with that carriage," I badgered him, and he'd mimic me over and over in an obnoxious voice, *"You be very careful. You be very careful. You be very careful."*

Maybe I was a little jealous that Mark liked it more when Carey took over, but *I* was responsible. I was the oldest.

"You just be very careful with that casket," I said under my breath from the back of the limousine. "You just be very careful."

5:15 AM

I sat back down at the desk and reached again for Fitzgerald, but put *Gatsby* aside for sections of the Sunday Globe that were haphazardly piled on a chair.

I tried to get through the Ideas Section, but Rosie's last words kept distracting me. What did she mean when she said: *"You have before, and forgotten that too."* Why did I not ask? Was I "the man who pretended to know everything?"

No.

How did this old drunken bag lady read me so well? I'd spent the entire afternoon the day before with my cousin Pam, who'd known me all my life, and even though she was only a few feet across the table, I couldn't have felt more alone. How is it that, at times, the people closest to you, can know you the very least?

Silence…

"Are you blaming yourself, Julien?" said Pam as soon as we found seats at the hotel bar while waiting for a table.

I thought: *Blame?* For a moment, my body pulsed with the very same detached horror of that morning 11 months earlier, when I'd paced back and forth on the dusty floor of my mother's attic beneath Mark's suspended body.

I didn't kill him. I didn't kill him. I didn't kill him…

I studied my fingers, then the three rows of suture marks crisscrossing the inside of my right wrist. "Are blame and contribution one and the same?" I said softly.

"What?" Pam said, and then rolled her eyes. "Oh, you know what I mean."

The talcum-sweetness of Shalimar, a signature scent she'd borrowed from our grandmother, hung in my mustache like a light dusting of powdered sugar. Whenever I am taken by that fragrance I am transported to my Grandmother Innes's dresser in the bedroom of her townhouse on Commonwealth Avenue where she'd lived all 93 years of her life. Standing among the lace and African violets I look past the crystal and sterling toiletries and see a much younger version of me staring back from the matching oak mirror.

Pam ordered an extra spicy Boody Mary with horseradish on the side. The bartender was very busy, but smiled professionally at her detailed instructions.

"Oh, wait," she called after him. "Lemon and lime please... thanks! And could you just put them both on a toothpick and not squeeze them."

I shook my head trying to look annoyed and amused at the same time while staring down at the gleaming brass rail at my feet that ran the length of the old mahogany bar.

"What?" she said, trying to catch my eye. "I like to squeeze it myself. I only like a little lime."

Her hair color of late was a hennaed brown, streaked with red highlights; the combination flattered her large brown eyes and pale Celtic complexion, unlike the purple streaks she was sporting a few months before. Her bangs were quite long, even for her, and they came straight across two carefully plucked brows in a precisely clipped line. They swayed from side to side like a tiny theater curtain closing as she turned swiftly toward me and slapped a few dollars on the bar for a tip.

"You know, Jules," she said, "there *is* a silver lining. It's always important to remember that."

"Geez, Pam," I said. "That was beautiful."

"I mean it," she said, and then lowered her voice to a very serious tone. "*I know this,*" she said, raising the top corner of her plumb-colored lips in a fashion she also used for sarcastic remarks.

We were called to our table — the menus still down when she was already on to the main course.

"Are you expressing any of your anger?" she asked with the calculated compassion of a talk show host. "How are you getting outside of yourself?"

My cousin has been a member of more twelve-step programs than I ever knew existed, though the only thing she's ever been addicted to besides drama, was psychobabble. At that moment a stab of loneliness shot through me, so sharp it felt like a kind of betrayal.

When I tried to look at my life in those days it was like viewing a strip of film all blurred and full of holes as though burned from being too close to the projecting light. And there I was, alone in my dark little theater, waiting for the film to resume.

Our plates arrived and the food instantly took center stage: steaming hot apple and cinnamon bread, poached eggs piled high on thinly-sliced, rare roast beef and running over in a smooth golden béarnaise, fried potatoes laced with basil and rosemary and garlic — dusted with paprika and all garnished with fresh melon and berries. We ate in merciful silence.

Rough, murky waves swelled in the harbor. Rain had been predicted for most of the day. By mid-afternoon the overhanging clouds had done nothing but hover heavily, casting a gray pallor over the sea. The muted light reflected off the water and made the earthy browns and greens embroidered into the tapestry of the drapes and chairs appear washed out and dull.

I watched the tug- and fishing boats shifting restlessly on the dark waves like tethered wild animals.

I related more with them than any of Pam's words of

comfort or, dare I say, advice as I felt bound and deserted too, strapped to my seat in my dark little theater.

She sat pushing a piece of apple bread around her plate and raised her head when she felt my eyes on her. She seemed to be hoping for some type of breakthrough to happen. Pamela never came close to the dark side of her own soul, though she loved to search those that belonged to anyone else.

We continued to eat in silence and when I was almost done I watched her again, this time unnoticed as she tilted her head absentmindedly off to the side of the table. I felt a warm rush of comfort that was not an unfamiliar feeling to associate with Pam, but surprised me just the same. She half-held her fork and began to tap it lightly with her index finger; this meant she was done. Then she reached over and squeezed my forearm just as our waiter miraculously appeared to remove our plates.

"You know it's O.K. to be mad at him." She said "O.K." slowly — in perfect synch with two overly sympathetic nods. I imagined her rehearsing this all morning in the mirror.

She went to acting school once, for about a week.

I didn't respond.

The waiter, a heavy-set man of about fifty, stood stock still beside the table as if waiting for my reaction as well.

"I'm all set," I said to him, and then quickly to her, "You don't want anything else, do you?"

She withdrew her hand from my arm as if contact with me had suddenly become painful.

"Just the check, please," I said, and he disappeared into the kitchen with our dirty plates.

"Look," I said. "I don't mean to be in such a rush, but I have to work later and I could really use a nap."

She held up both hands in front of her as if telling *me* enough is enough.

"O.K. All right," she said. "I just want to make sure

you're getting outside yourself. You know, coming from an alcoholic family you're just bound to have some trouble with your feelings."

Trouble with my feelings? I felt like saying: "Sweetheart, you couldn't spell the things I feel. There are no words."

I no more wanted to hurt her than I had any desire to share any of my "feelings" with her, so I said nothing and rearranged myself in my chair. The rear cushion was broad, but not tall enough for my long physique, and a dull ache had begun in my lower back. I tried very hard to look as though I were waiting patiently for the check.

I love my cousin. She is genuinely kind and we have always been close as we are nearly the same age and grew up together.

But here was a woman who at thirty had been married three times. The year before Mark died she had sat on the sofa in my apartment in Cambridge, crying crocodile tears into her diamond and emerald weighted fingers, explaining how she planned to save her third marriage:

"I know Nathan is a trust fund kid and has never worked a day in his life. I accept that he's a drug addict, too. So, that makes him a pathological liar and a thief. And yes, I know he's gay — *sometimes*. But I love him, Julien. Nathan and I will make it work."

Well, after the marriage dissolved, she went into counseling and moved maybe a fraction of an inch in therapy and has since been on a crusade to heal the rest of the world, anyone but herself.

"You know," I said letting my exhaustion fill my face from across the table, "I don't know what the hell I feel most days. The only way I feel right now is tired. All I can think of is a nap."

"Well you should feel a little... *Something*," she said. "It's been a year almost. And you're isolating yourself, Julien. You live like a hermit in that one-room hovel. Gave up that great place in Porter Square. Then you just quit your job — a great job."

I wouldn't attempt to explain that I'd rather be helping some drunk out of urine-soaked pants, than trying to pacify some irate customer at the restaurant I had managed. You know, that character disorder who wants the entire check comped because his prime rib was not rare enough, or whose Caesar salad was late.

Now *she* stared out the window; the look on her face was one of disbelief. "You never should have moved out of that place or left your job so abruptly. You had great rent, a great salary."

"Are you done?" I asked, forcing a grin. I was digging deeply for some good humor which disappeared promptly with her response:

"Yes," she said in a meek, low voice. Then she pursed her lips into the imitation smile I'd seen her flash thousands of times over the years at people like her father, or one of her husbands, when she was failing at some manipulative strategy and wanted to feign a coy surrender.

"Look, I just need some…" I raised two fingers on each hand and made quote marks in the air, "… space." I realized now that the conversation had gone precisely where I'd tried in earnest to avoid. "And I'm doing fine, really. I mean, if my bills are paid and I have enough money left over for ramen noodles and cigarettes, then everything is cool."

She took a breath to speak, but I continued, "And since when do other people's decisions have to make sense to you, anyway?"

She had no answer for that. The check came and as I reached for my wallet her hand came back across the table and gave my arm another gentle squeeze. "This is on me," she said, tilting her chin forward as if to support the weight of her eyes now pouring over with more misplaced sympathy.

"No, really. It's O.K. I..."

"No, *you* look," she said. "It's simple: I have a lot of money. You have none. There are a few perks to being a professional wife."

I laughed because I knew she believed that to be true, but by the time we were walking through the cocktail lounge and toward the elevator, I was eyeing the room for clearly marked exits.

"Hey, Pam," I said, seeing my chance, "I'm going to walk, if you don't mind. I really could use some air."

"Fine," she said tersely. "I'm just worried about you, Julien. Everyone is."

"What do you mean *everyone?*" I felt a rush of heat to my cheeks. Then I was just annoyed. "I'm fine, Pam. Don't worry."

"Your mother says she never sees you."

"That's not true," I said. "She was just used to seeing me *all* the time, for a while there."

But it was true. As the months had passed I found myself going to my mother's house less and less. So much seemed missing as if all the paintings had been taken down from the walls and everywhere I looked there were big empty spaces to which my eyes couldn't adjust.

"I work nights," I said "She works days. It's difficult."

Pam was not that easily swayed. "Carey says you don't ever call him, or even return his calls. I can relate."

The elevator arrived and we rode two floors down to the ground level in the quiet, crowded car.

As we walked through the lobby beneath the tall ficus and palm trees that stood in enormous pots of hammered copper and Chinese porcelain, I didn't even want to look at her for fear she'd begin again. The heat on that floor was oppressive.

She began to walk with me out to the street and, knowing she'd parked in the garage, I didn't object or try to stop for good-byes. I didn't want to seem any more eager than I was already to just get away.

It had just begun to rain and the sidewalk was mottled into pasty black and slate blue, the way it is only before being completely saturated with raindrops.

We picked up our pace, mine more brisk than hers. She lagged a bit behind me, the way reporters on the eleven o'clock news follow people with microphones as they come out of their homes, or work, or court, and I laughed a bit. Just a snicker, but enough to cue Pam.

She stepped back into an alcove that framed two wide service doors with no handles on the outside. I stopped too, but remained under the rain with no intention of being stationary long.

"What the hell is so funny?" she said, wounded. "You always think everything is so humorous." Injured, she folded both arms high on her chest and tucked her purse beneath them. "It's all very funny, isn't it, that everyone tries and tries to reach you, and you just chuckle and move further and further away. *Push* further away, I should say."

"It's not like that." I stepped beneath the threshold, leaning with one shoulder against the opposite wall. "It's not that I..."

"No man is an island." She pointed one finger up in the air, but toward me.

If someone had told me she was going to say exactly that I simply wouldn't have believed it. And she made it sound as if it were her own brilliant insight, not John Donne's.

"Carey needs his big brother now," she said.

A fury rose through my neck as if forced by some now riotous blaze that had smoldered all afternoon — all year. Had she not been staring past me and blankly over the Atlantic Avenue traffic, she would have seen it coming sooner.

"Pamela, what the fuck do you know about anything?" I said it so low and mean that it made her bottom lip quiver.

I can't take tears, even Pam's fake ones. They remind me all too well of the real ones, I suppose. But the bottom lip thing couldn't be faked. Ordinarily that alone would make me not only lay down my arms right there but run out and buy her some flowers as well. But this time I didn't care. Not since the days before I'd stopped drinking had I felt such a loss of control.

"What the Christ do you have to tell me about rising to anything?" I said. "What the hell goes through your head, anyway? Do you think you can spout what you heard about suicide on fucking Dr. Phil, then pick up the check? Let's move on to coffee and dessert now. and you'll have saved my life? That it will be last spring again? What do *you* have to impart to *me*? The only thing of value you ever lost was a diamond fucking bracelet."

"And three husbands," she said, her voice cracking like a tiny glass bulb, signaling a point I would have never before gone beyond. But still, I didn't care.

"Of value!" I said without flinching.

Her eyes darted, more frightened than hurt.

"Don't you get *anything*? I have absolutely nothing to say that you want to hear," I said, seeing authentic tears swell under her long lashes.

"But I'll tell you anyway. Do you think you can point your perfect little nails at me and say I've got to find a silver lining?"

She moved away from me, shoulders caving forward in crushed defeat. I shot to the other side, directly in front of her, and tried to catch her eyes again.

"Do you remember all those years when I was so fucked up?" I said, quickly grabbing my wrist and holding it tightly with my other hand. She moved back and winced. "Do you think I 'got outside of myself' then?"

Now her tears spilled over, mascara-stained streaks down either cheek.

"That was a long time ago, Julien," she said with a quality in her voice that sounded as if she were defending herself. Looking back I sense that voice coming from a very deep and loyal place. At the time, however, it had no endearing effect on me.

"You can't feel guilty," she said. "You were a good brother to Mark — the best." She swabbed either side of her face with the back of a shaking hand. "You had to be both father and brother to him, and it wasn't fair." She wiped at her face again, and searched through her purse for a Kleenex. "Besides," she said, as if it had only just then occurred to her, "you were a little messed up for a while, that's all. You haven't even touched a drink for almost ten years." Gesturing to my sleeve, she added, "I don't think about those days anymore. "No one else does, either."

"Do I care what the hell *you* or *anyone* else thinks? You think I sit in my 'hovel' all day and ruminate over how anyone perceives me?" I started to laugh again, but it was a bit spastic, almost sinister.

"You of all people should know how bad it had been between me and Mark when he died." I was practically shouting. "What could you possibly have to tell me about what kind of a brother I was, or am now, for that matter?"

She kept her head down and inhaled in short, stuttering gasps. Utterly speechless, she refused to look at me. I looked over her head to the door without handles.

"Hey," I said, grabbing her by both of her shoulders. Still she avoided eye contact. "Do... not... worry, O.K.?" I kissed the top of her head, stepped backward into the rain, turned, and walked away.

"Screw you Julien," she muttered through a voice drenched with more genuine tears, "Screw you."

Silence...

The last time Mark and I spoke was on the phone

about a week before he died. He'd finished high school a few months prior. Since his sophomore year he'd worked as an assistant to a neighborhood plumber and, man, he loved that job. He wanted to learn the trade, but he was "laid off" just after graduation, for not being able to "keep up," his boss had said.

Mark had a slight learning disability which, to some extent, affected his motor control and coordination. I encouraged him to learn and work as hard as he could, but was afraid that the finer, more technical points of plumbing could be a problem. I hoped he'd get by with complete determination, that he'd found his niche, that he'd be one of *those* stories.

But it *was* a problem. He had always been in Special Ed, and it was never a major concern. But, when he lost that job, and had so much trouble finding another, I could see for the first time what a number that did on him.

After losing the plumbing job he took a truck-driving course and failed the test twice. I aided him as best I could. Did job searches for him and offered to help outline his driver's manual and study again for the test. Every offer was rebuffed, out of what I saw as a mix of anger, frustration, and pride. So I backed off.

But this day I called him because my mother had called me. She was worried that he wasn't working after so many months, and had reached a point where he all but refused to even look for a job.

He had also taken to disappearing for days at a time. Without word, he'd show up for a change in clothes, or a random meal. My mother pleaded with him at least to let her know when he would, or wouldn't be returning.

"Who the hell do you think you are?" I yelled into the receiver. "Mom's home is not a flop house, you know? She put me out, and she'll throw your ass out as well if you don't stop acting like a complete loser."

There was no reply but the sound of his breathing.

"Get your shit together!" I said, and slammed down the receiver with more fury than I'd dialed it.

That night my mother called me and said when she came in from work she went to his room and found him awake, just lying there in the dark. She said she could tell he'd been crying, and when she asked him what was wrong, all he said was, "Even Julien thinks I'm a loser."

Silence...

5:32 AM

I glanced at the clock. It wasn't yet time for the clipboard checklist. So I picked up the newspaper and tried to read an article on the impending phone company strike. I had to start it three times. But the thought of him lying there in the dark, crying. *How could he have possibly believed, even for a moment, that I had such a little opinion of him?*

If only I had recognized that sign for what it was, to indicate what he was going to do; if he'd come out and actually said something — slipped up, even. Was I not always the one who read others so well? If he'd actually given me the chance.

What had Rosie said earlier? "You don't see? He's telling you he knows quite well that you would have tried to help him if you'd had the chance. He's saying that he knows you could have, and quite easily taken care of it, too."

I knew what it was like to be a kid and believe in all that hurts and disappoints you — everything that makes you doubt.

I also knew how easy it was for a kid to doubt because a teenager has nothing to hold it all up against, nothing that hadn't been viewed through a child's eye, anyway. And how it all seems so out of our control which is why we take it out on ourselves, whether we are aware of it or not. It's self-controlling the misery — or at least some of it.

Silence...

He called me in the morning on a Sunday and, though it was not uncommon for him to make an impromptu call to see if I wanted to hang out, it was unusual of late.

In the years after Dad left, and Mom was working and going to school nights, the three of us — Mark, Corey and I — became very close and spent a lot of time together. But I had this fear that when Mark and Carey got older they would resent me as teens often do their parents. I mean, I knew very well that I was not a parent, and I really didn't try to be, either, but the fact was I had to assume the role — at times. And I was afraid they would resent me even more precisely because I was *not* their father,

After all, I was the one who had to make sure they were home on time and got their homework done, and scolded them sometimes for being wise asses or acting up, and settled tiffs between them. I especially made time to get to their baseball and soccer games, and take them to judo class or to the movies or out for pizza in the North End. Sometimes we would just go for a cruise around town, or out along the north shore beaches and just listen to the radio while tooling around together. They loved that, and I did too. Even if I were just running errands, they would want to tag along, and I liked to oblige.

They came to rely on me for things such as help with homework, or a ride to a friend's, a few extra bucks or, on that rare occasion, dare I say, advice. They respected me, too, in the way that children respect authority figures, mostly letting me believe they were listening when I spoke and not giving me lip when they knew I was really angry.

Nevertheless, I wondered if they were suddenly going to wake up one day and realize that I was not an authority figure at all, that I didn't really know much more than they ever did — and who did I think I was to tell them anything? Where the hell did I get off?

The resentment certainly kicked in for Carey during

that period when I got so messed up and was drinking all the time. He didn't cut me any slack then. After all, I was his big brother; he relied on me to be there and to keep him in-line, not the other way around. He just could not forgive me for dropping the ball and not doing the job I had agreed to take on.

I know it bothered Mark in those days as well, but he was pretty silent. He was really too young. His adolescent rebellion simmered under the surface until the months after he graduated high school, when he was having a hard time finding work and passing the truck drivers' test. I could hardly engage him in a conversation, let alone get him to spend time with me. *Give him some space,* I told myself. *He'll get over it and will come back around in the future.*

I thought that by *not* trying to help, I was giving him what he needed.

So I was surprised to get his call out of the blue on that Sunday morning a few weeks before he died. He asked what I was up to, if I wanted to hang out. I couldn't remember the last time he'd done that, but I was all too happy that he did.

It was such a nice day we wandered around the city without any itinerary at all. Driving down by the Esplanade along Storrow, we looked for my friend Harry's football game without much luck, and then cruised up to Harvard Square and got an ice cream. It was the first part of October and still warm, and The Square was filled with people and street performers and music. Fall had not yet hit, and it was as though everyone were sure that all the warm days would be gone after this, and they were all out and reaching for that one last chance.

Later in the day I was going to take him back to my mother's house for Sunday dinner and, in those last few hours we spent together sitting on my front stoop in Porter Square, I remember him seeming pensive, almost apprehensive. But I quickly dismissed the thought.

A friend stopped by and we all hung out for a while. When I casually asked if she wanted to come along with us, I caught this look on his face as though he had just recovered from brief but potent disappointment. I dismissed that too; we were having such a nice time sitting there talking and laughing and watching the passers-by.

Now it just seems so, I don't know, poignant — or perhaps apparent is a better word, but only with the luxury of retrospect. Looking back, I can't help but feel as though he were trying to say something to me. Did he spend that entire day trying to get up the courage to ask me for help? Did he call me that morning because I was his last hope, and then I simply brushed him off?

5:52AM

I went into the kitchen to fire a pot of java. There was still coffee in the pot so I just nuked some in the largest mug I could find.

Two other incidents kept coming back to me at seemingly arbitrary times, but with a certain strength that night. I didn't really wonder why, but found myself going over them again as I stared at the microwave waiting for the coffee.

These occasions didn't have any particular meaning when they happened. But afterward — after Mark died, that is — when I looked at them, then, they seemed like messages he was trying to send me, a celestial tap on my shoulder to remind me not necessarily of who I believed I was, but perhaps how he saw me?

One was a Ricky Lee Jones concert, nothing out of the ordinary as music venues go; and the other a simple sandwich.

I was always very passionate about music and I remember him as a little kid and how he would always come in my room and sit on my bed when I was in there playing music. I can see him now, five or six years-old, singing along to a Talking Heads or Pretenders song while he flips through album covers and looks at lyrics and artwork and asks me about them. He wanted to know things like if "Psycho Killer" were about a real murderer and if he killed people for not being polite, and who were the people on the cover of *Sargent Pepper's*. When he got older, and I wasn't home, I let him use my stereo as long as he took care of it and, even though every now and then there were new scratches on certain records and an occasional broken needle, I never took that privilege away from him.

The truth was that I would have broken as many needles and eventually hacked up every LP I owned, and I loved to come home and find him sitting on my bed by himself with my headphones on and a Rolling Stones or Led Zeppelin cover on his lap. He told me once, when he was about 11 or 12, that I was the coolest brother for two reasons: not only because I had the best music collection in the world, but also because I let him use my stereo whenever I wasn't around. None of his other friends' brothers or parents would ever let them near their stereo equipment.

At any rate, he could sing Rickie Lee's "Danny's All-Star Joint" word-for-word before he knew his multiplication tables. We were driving one day, I don't even recall where, but it was in the year before he died. Anyway, "Chuck E.'s in Love" came on the radio and he recalled that I had taken him to see her at an outside show a few summers before. Then, he mentioned, rather off-handedly, that it had been the first — and last — concert he ever went to. I was stunned. I had seen so many shows by the time I was 19. I remember thinking: *Shit, I was in the Boston Garden at Alice Cooper the summer before my first year of high school.*

I couldn't believe that he had never been to any other shows, and I remember saying something like, "You know, you better hurry up because you got some music to experience." But, all in all, it didn't really seem that significant at the time. All I can think now is: *Wow. Taking someone to their first show is somewhat of an honor. But, bringing someone to the only concert they will ever attend for their entire life is something else altogether.*

And then there was that afternoon, a few months before he died, when I was at my mother's house and made myself a sandwich. What could be less-significant than that? He hadn't had much to say, as was the deal of late, but emerged from the family room where he was watching a movie and came right over and sat down at the table and just stared at me. At first I thought: *Cool.* But when I tried to engage him, I got his short one-word answers until there was a long pause and he only looked at the sandwich, and then back at me.

I asked if he would like a bite, then cut off a quarter and handed to him.

"Ha!" he said as though he had just proven me wrong on something and, when I looked back at him, he just smiled. "All my life I've been able to do that," he said, and shook his head .

"Do what?" I asked, a bit too resentfully.

"All my life, if you made something to eat, and you always make the best sandwiches, all I have to do is sit down and look like I *might* want some. I don't even have to ask. Sure enough, I mean I could put money on it, you'd cut off a nice piece and just fork it right over to me."

"Oh," I said, irked. He seemed so arrogant at that moment — as though he were so sure in his infinite adolescent wisdom and saw right through me. "Wow, you really have me pegged. Because I'm such a sucker, right?"

"No," he said between chewing, and pausing to swallow, "Because you're so generous."

6:14AM

A sudden, loud crash sounded like someone or something was ramming the front wall of the church. I leapt from my chair, sending what was left of my coffee spraying all over my lap and the top of the desk.

"What the hell!" I shouted into the darkness. I fumbled for the rolling mug while imagining someone storming through the doors beneath the front stair case. Shit. Did I check those after my first rounds? After the police left? Claudia?

The vibrations from the crash still resounded in my chest as I hurdled the steps, stage left, and ran up the aisle to the back of the men's dorm.

I moved fast, but cautiously in the dark and was at the far end in seconds where a few dark figures were gathered by the last beds. I noticed some noise, like the beating of enormous wings: swish-swoosh, swish-swoosh. For an instant I thought of Rosie's angel as I tried to follow the sound through the thick shapes of shoulders and legs huddled in the shadows; *swish-swoosh, swish swoosh.*

An older man in sweat pants, someone to whom I'd given the key when I came out of the kitchen, stood in the doorway of the men's bathroom. He held the door opened wide, and I could see Stanley lying on his side in the brash block of fluorescent light. His huge body slid wildly back and forth in one shuddering convulsion after another.

Winston and Sampson, among a few others, stood over him, motionless.

"Don't anyone try and help him, now," I said, pushing

past them.

"Oh, please," spewed Wilson, breaking his empty gaze with a disgusted smirk for me. "None of you people know anything. This asshole here woke me up."

I immediately got down beside Stanley and grabbed his jerking head, sliding my knees beneath it. I took a firm hold of his shoulders, and his entire upper body lunged forward like a wild bronco in one great heave, sending me smashing into the metal frame of his bed. I recovered quickly, rolling right back over to the same position and pulled his head back to my lap, trying to force open his mouth with my fingers

The only time I'd ever seen a person have a convulsion was back in college. During a psychology lecture, this guy a few seats from me started choking. I watched as his body jerked in violent shudders and spit ran down his chin and neck.

The professor ran over and pulled a small memo book from his breast pocket and jammed it between the kid's teeth. The teacher explained later it was a precaution to prevent him from biting or swallowing his tongue. That stayed with me, I don't know why. Some years after that night at the shelter, while recounting this event, a paramedic friend of mine politely assured me that putting your hand in the mouth of someone having a seizure is a sure-fire way of losing some fingers. Also, the idea that the person is swallowing his tongue is false, and one should never insert anything into the patient's mouth. I really could have used that advice *beforehand* as I really had no time to look up any seizure-first-aid procedures.

Stanley's hot and sour breath came in deep gasps between his iron-clenched jaws as I pried them apart. Thick, sticky saliva sprayed out over my hands and forearms. I wedged them open, jammed the corner of my fist into the side, and reached around for my wallet. I forced the billfold past his teeth and he bit down hard, but the leather immediately slipped out the side and his molars caught the tip of my ring finger.

"Motherfucker!" I screamed and grabbed him by his bottom jaw with all my might and, careful of my bleeding finger, lodged the wallet back inside his mouth.

Someone from the women's side was shouting something about how I should watch my mouth and treat people like human beings.

I could see blood streaked up the inside of my arm. I wasn't sure whether it was his or mine.

By the time the wallet was in a second time, Stanley's arms and legs had stopped flailing, and now they twitched only slightly as if from tiny, uncontrollable waves of an electrical current. His breathing became steadier. Sampson, the only spectator left, now crouched beside me. Even the guy holding the bathroom door had lost interest and let it close with a quiet thud, leaving us again in the shadows.

"Is he O.K.?" Sampson asked. "Will he be alright?" I didn't answer right away and he stared at me for a moment, his permanently wrinkled brow crumpling even more.

"He'll be all right," I said.

The metal frames of the small window high on the basement wall beside us, which for hours had bordered a solid patch of black, now held a slowly brightening rectangle of blue. Stanley, Sampson, and I sat in the soft, quietly receding darkness of the approaching dawn.

I looked back to Stanley and immediately became aware of the tremendous heat coming from his head. I yanked my hands back.

Enormous, grimy, fingers came from his side and grabbed at the wallet in his mouth. He sucked some of the spit from the sides as he slowly pulled it out, then gathered up something in his mouth as if it were a dislodged tooth and spit it in a bloodied pool of saliva on the floor. He wiped my wallet on his shirt, careful to get all sides, and handed it back to me.

"Thanks," he said in a low grunt, and sat up. In the growing light from the window I saw the cut on his forehead; not too clearly, mostly just smudged streaks of red across his forehead, and down one side of his face. My own wound, which I assumed to be a puncture at the top of my finger, was hidden beneath a gooey coating of blood which looked as if it had already started to thicken.

My hand throbbed a bit, but didn't really hurt that much, so I tried to examine Stanley's gash more closely. He sat still, leaning on one arm and holding the back of his neck with the other.

He raised his matted head slowly as if trying to recall, or hear, something. I backed away, and he put his hand to his forehead, running his fingers over the area above the bridge of his nose and looked at them as if to figure out the cause of the wetness he found there. Then he shifted toward me in a sharp turn as if I'd surprised him.

"Are you O.K., Stanley?"

"Fine!" he shouted and dropped his face to the floor. I had never before heard him raise his voice. Usually he hardly made any sounds at all, except an occasional "Hey" when he passed.

After a few seconds, sweat and blood began to roll down from his face and over his nose, in a slow, steady, spiral. The drips then fell away from one another as his head twitched, spreading in tiny black balloons on the cement floor.

He shifted again, and tilted his head.

"Get out!" He said in a vicious, but very defensive voice,. Then he leaned closer to me and said with even more ferocity: "Put my mitt back and get out of my room. NOW! Or I'm gonna call Mom. Now!"

I retreated even more; Sampson did the same. I didn't want to look at Stanley just then. I don't know if I felt embarrassed or afraid. I followed the uneven surface of the cement floor, stopping at the black shining globs of blood.

"GET OUT NOW!" He yelled again, and then covered his ears. The beads of sweat and blood did not cascade unevenly now, but flew off his cheeks and chin as he spoke, as though little pieces of him flew loose.

"What do you do for two freaking minutes of sleep in this dump, huh?" a woman muttered as she passed the end of the men's dorm on her way to the water cooler over by the laundry door.

Sampson grew nearer and crouched over again. He watched Stanley closely, but without alarm.

"Aw, give him his baseball mitt back, Jules," he said. "You have another one don't you? You can buy one when you get paid, can't you? Why did you take his anyway, huh?"

Stanley was a kid?
Stanley was a kid.

He had a bedroom. *Was it messy most of the time, like mine? Did he have a GI Joe or Leggos or any posters on his walls?*

"I don't have his baseball glove, Sampson," I said.

I got behind Stanley on the floor. Putting both arms under his I said, "Come on pal... up." He nodded, and slowly stood with me.

"We need to take a look at your forehead," I said. "Let's go in here a minute," and motioned him toward the men's room. Sampson followed.

My finger didn't seem to be bleeding any more so I decided to sort Stanley out first. Squinting under the harsh light at the sink I could see his cut wasn't as deep as all the blood made it appear.

I poked Sampson with my elbow, "Get me a clean towel from the closet, O.K.?"

He turned quickly to walk away, then stopped. "Are you gonna give him his mitt?" he said.

"No, I'm not. Will you just go? Please?"

Stanley was moving pretty well now. He leaned

against the tiled wall beside the mirror as I started running the hot water. Before the sink was even full, Sampson was back, holding out a faded blue towel.

"Do me a favor?" I said, taking the towel from him.

His eyes widened and he smiled eagerly. "Sure, anything you want. Anything you want, I'll do for you. Just ask me Julien and I'll…"

"O.K. O.K. O.K.," I said. "You know the desk where I sit? Go to the box on the wall just behind it — the big white box with the light switches. You know?"

He shook his head up and down enthusiastically.

"All right, then. Turn every one of them on, one at a time." I was thinking I could go back and turn off all the exterior lights afterward.

Sam was out the door.

I checked my watch. *Six forty-seven—Shoot. They should have been on at six thirty.*

I bunched up one corner of a towel and soaked it with hot water, pumped shiny pink hand soap into it and rubbed the liquid into the cloth. Stanley stood straight and held his shoulders back as if ready for an inspection, his eyes squeezed shut. His whole body seemed to flinch at the first touch of my hand when I brought the towel to his face,but then remained ridgedly still. Soon I loosened dried blood and grime into a dark amber film and wiped the streaks away with the dry side of the towel.

I swiped his forehead with the wet end and followed the deep creases and pock marks down from his thick, low hair line to just above his eyes. They were opened wide now and I could see how brown they were; a deep, dark mahogany that held me. I was pulled into their depths by something very fragile, like an infant's hand gripping my finger.

Who defeated *you?*

Where is the boy who ever chased after a ball, or delivered a newspaper, or ordered his brother out of his room?

And for a moment I saw Stanley the way maybe only our mothers ever see us, before anything happened to us. When we were without blame.

I could see quite clearly how he hadn't put himself beneath my hands at that moment, or even on that floor moments before, or at the shelter, or in prison, or on the streets. Somewhere, something had been taken from him; stolen, more likely.

He raised one of his massive hands to wipe at a matted clump of mucky hair stuck to his right ear. He trembled so that it took a few swipes before he freed it completely.

I stood unable to move. I was speechless, and felt a constriction in my throat as though something were about rise and I, skillfully at this point, forced it back.

How was it that this indigent brute, this murderer, conjured such emotion in me? Was it simply because he was allowing me to help him, to touch his face?

An inferno blazed deep within me, then was gone — blown out by the draft from the swinging door — kicked open with a hollow smack from the bottom of Winston's boot. He stepped in coolly, both hands in the pockets of his dingy jeans. I grabbed him by the shoulders of his stained tee shirt and threw his emaciated frame against the tiled wall.

"What the hell is wrong with you?"

Stunned at first, Winston gathered himself, grinning, proud of making me lose my cool.

"Easy, buddy," he said. "Job got you a little stressed out?" Then he laughed and his hot, putrid breath hit my face. I let go of him more out of disgust than fear that something regrettable might happen.

I turned to the thud of the door as it closed by itself, Stanley on the other side.

Winston pretended to fix his disheveled self in the

mirror, running his fingers over the collar of his tee shirt and spreading the material flat across his chest.

"You know, you don't want to go grabbing the wrong person, now," he said, and sneered again while going into one of the stalls as Sampson came busting through the door all wide-eyed and eager.

"I put all the lights on, Jules," he said. "I put on every one just like you said. Then I got out a whole bunch of clean towels on the table nice. Just like you do in two stacks, just like you."

"Thanks, Sam," I said, letting the sudsy, clouded water drain from the sink. "Do me another favor while I clean myself up?"

"Sure. I can do anything you want. Just ask. Just ask."

"All right. Look," I said, holding up one key on my ring. "Can you take this key, and open the alley door with it?"

"Sure I can, just for you."

"You have to turn it two times, and kick the dead bolt over with your foot, got it?" I said, not letting go of the key as he grabbed at it a few times.

"I can do that for you, no problem. I'll do it just for you."

"Hey, I got something in here just for you, you little fucking retard," Winston snickered from the stall. "Come in here, you pain in the ass, and I'll show you."

Sam's face never moved from mine, nor did it register that he heard any of Winston's insults.

"And put them right back in my hand immediately after," I said. I held my hand open and he seized the key and ran out the door.

"Slow down," I called after him, and began rinsing the sink and filling it again with more hot water when Winston emerged from the stall, no sound of the toilet flushing behind him. He walked toward the sinks and I followed him in the mirror, hoping he would trip.

"Naw, you ain't scared of that little prick scheming anything with your keys. He's much too stupid for that," Winston said with a sinister cackle. "But he would drive a saint to drink with that fucking voice alone. Hell," he said as if it were an afterthought, "If I was his mother, I'd a lit his ass on fire too."

"What?" I said.

"I mean, couldn't you see it? Coming home after a good tear and him coming after you, begging you every day for shit, in that freaking retarded voice?"

He smiled again proudly, this time showing me all of his gray gums. What he said almost didn't register. It was like a punch that left me winded, and too numb to feel. I tried to dispel it as a mean lie, or a rumor.

"Yup," he said, as if he were bragging, and flattened down the greasy hair at his ears. "I knew his old lady years ago. His father, too."

He paused and moved closer into my mirror. At once I was in a place I desperately wanted to leave but was paralyzed until he continued to speak. He rubbed the stubble on his chin and turned from side to side while examining his jaw.

"They used to drink down at the Light House Lounge. Back then you could get a draft beer for a quarter." He stopped and looked at my reflection in the mirror. Was I supposed to be impressed he'd been a fucking dive barfly that long?

"Anyway, he was a junkie, and she was drunk the whole time she was knocked- up. After she had the kid, she was stuck home and that's when she started booting junk too, and was always after the old man to cop for her." He tucked in his tee shirt and looked directly at me in the mirror.

"He always complained about them being dead weights around his neck, and that someday he was gonna sink 'em both in the Charles." Winston laughed again, then sauntered over to the door.

"He'd have done well doing just that, cuz now she's doing life instead for killing him, and trying to eighty-six the retard as well. Shit," he said, sneering, "She stabbed him in his sleep one night, tied them both to a bed, and torched it. She turned up a few days later and said she was so high she didn't remember anything. Somehow the kid got free. His testimony put her away, though. Should of tied a tighter knot is what I say."

Silence...

6:42 AM

After Winston left, I had the mirror to myself. All I could think about his tale was: How does anyone survive *that*? What capacity does the human heart have for suffering?

I remembered Sampson's version, and was taken aback by the resourcefulness of his lie. He couldn't even beat me at Old Maid on his own, yet he figured out a perfect story? I mean, I bought it right off. Never even questioned it, or him.

My mouth was gaping. I had to put my eyes elsewhere, and down at my hand.

Most of the blood on my fingers had been rinsed away when I cleaned off Stanley. A deep red scab seemed to be forming at the top. After a wash with warm soapy water I saw that an entire half of the tip was gone — even a piece of the nail. It wasn't bleeding anymore and looked almost cauterized, as if by a hot iron.

Then I remembered Stanley spitting out something. "Holy shit!" I wondered, *should I go back and look for it?* "Maybe they can sew it back on," I said to the mirror in a sarcastic, perky optimism. Then I started laughing hard. Really hard.

I stared at my reflection and, still laughing, said, "You have to get out of here." Then, as if completely out of my own control, my face instantly recovered and was earnestly serious. "You have to get the fuck out of here," I said.

6:57 AM

I had just finished dousing my finger with peroxide from the first aid box and was wrapping it tightly in gauze and tape, when Kyle entered, stage left.

He put his briefcase on the desk and gently squeezed the sides of his Styrofoam coffee cup. He lifted the lid and blew on it before taking a quick sip, still not looking directly at me.

"How was your night?"

"Fine," I said.

"No problems?"

"Just another day in the life, except..." I held up my bandaged hand.

"What the heck happened to you?"

"Oh it's nothing. Stanley had a seizure and bit me while I was trying help him. It's nothing. It really doesn't even hurt. I should have it checked anyway."

"Can I see it?" Kyle said, genuinely alarmed. "How deep is it?"

"It's not bad, really."

"What about Stanley?"

"He seems fine. He cut his forehead when he fell. Nothing serious. He took off after I cleaned it for him. I would have disinfected it too, but he was gone. Was he out in the alley when you came in?"

"No." he said. "But you have to have that looked at right away. Let me just put this stuff in my office and you can take off. Stephanie will be in any minute."

He looked at me over his glasses, and exited stage left for his office.

I tidied up the top of the desk and threw away yesterday's paper, now soggy from the spilled coffee, and grabbed a damp sponge from the kitchen to wipe down the dried streaks around the edge and on the front of the drawers and floor. People had begun to congregate in the recreation area and were coming and going from the alleyway.

Over by the office stairs, Sampson was trying to coax Andrea Alvarez out of a cigarette. She kept asking him if he was a cop, and he puffed out his chest at the compliment, but never strayed from the topic of the Lucky Strike she held in the air, just beyond his grasp.

I stretched my neck and it felt thick and sore. Watching Sam I felt as though I were now seeing him in a way that I shouldn't, a way in which I had no right. Winston's tale had done that to me.

He snatched the cigarette in the very second Andrea lowered it within his reach and bolted up to the stage.

"Hey Jules," he said and propped himself up on the side of the desk, cigarette tucked neatly behind a knotted ear. He picked up the log and quickly flipped through the pages.

"Gimme that," I said grabbing it from him. He flinched and shrank back a bit as if I were going to hit him. I put my hand on his shoulder, but his attention was down at his thigh where his hand fiddled uneasily with loose threads from a hole in his worn jeans. He seemed wounded. I'd never seen that side of him.

I was distressed that I might have hurt his feelings, which annoyed me at the same time, because I simply wanted to leave, and the whole interaction seemed insignificant. But also because I'd always assumed it was impossible to hurt Sampson's feelings. He didn't even get it when others *tried* to wound him. How the hell did I manage to do it?

His hand skittishly fingered the loose strands of denim unraveling around a hole the size of a nickel on his upper leg.

I wanted tell him: *These frayed threads are the same as the ones that bind us here — Now. We think we sew the fabric together, but there is a Master Tailor whose skilled needle knows ways we cannot fathom.*

Not me, who seeks but shall never know.

And not you, whose already poor house was slowly robbed blind throughout your very young life — then excavated, then leveled.

"Did anyone even notice, or look for something rising from the smoke and the rubble?" I said under my breath.

"What are you talkin' about? Rubble? Jules? Barney Rubble? I got to go. I got to go to see Linda. She's gonna get me a job. Do you wanna come with me to the T? Do you wanna come to the T-stop?"

"I can't," I said. "Not today. I've got to get on home."

"O.K., Jules. I'll see you tonight. I don't want to be late for Linda. Linda says people won't give me a job me if I'm late. I've got to get my train. I can't be late."

I felt bad as I watched him cross the rec area for the alley stairs. I knew then that I would not be back that night or any other.

"They are your eyes, Mr. Julien," Rosie said. She was fully dressed, with an old black straw hat pinned tightly to her head. On the brim was a crunched bouquet of faded silk flowers held on by bent wire.

They're mine?

"I've got to be off and get some balloons together. The weather man said that today is going to be beauteous. They'll be lots of strollers along The Common."

When she moved closer as if to tell me something in confidence I could smell the stale wine on her breath mixed up with the smoky staleness of her overcoat. I had the weird idea of buying her a bottle of nice perfume, and imagined mailing it to her at the shelter after I was gone, but then envisioned her waking in the middle of the night and drinking it.

"Sometimes she takes you where you don't necessarily *want* to go. But you always *need* to see what she's showing you. So, in the long run, it's not so bad," she said.

"I know," I said, referring to the part about it not being so bad, but she had already turned, and was walking away.

"Or it's to free you completely," she said peering back over her shoulder. Then a laugh came from deep in her throat, which quickly turned into a thick, gurgling cough. She was almost choking by the time she ascended the stairs, stopping to spit into a tissue she drew from the pocket of her coat.

Stephanie, my relief, nodded at Rosie as she passed her on the stairs. She was about twenty, diminutive and slight. When she first started working at the mission a few months prior I remembered thinking: *Oh they'll chew this one right up and spit her out.* But from what I could see she got on quite well as she sprang around like a stern, responsible baby-sitter.

"Hi Julien," she said. "How was your night?"

"Great," I said. "A cake-walk," keeping my hand from view.

She hung her coat and went into Kyle's office. I grabbed mine and headed for the door.

"Exit, stage right." I said for the last time.

7:08 AM

Preacher Jack stood beside the large opening beneath the wooden staircase, with his back to the hallway. He faced the brick wall of the original foundation — still charred black from the century-old fire. He held a tattered Bible in his left hand; it was closed on his index finger and pressed tightly to his chest. The other hand was opened and raised high over his head. His shadow stretched like smoke across the bricks in the morning light coming from the hall windows.

"And the King of Babylon ordered that these men be thrown into a furnace so hot that it slew the guards who delivered them into it. And the king was astounded at what he saw, and asked his men, 'Did we not throw three men into the flames?'

"And his counselors replied, 'True, oh King.'

"'But I see four men walking among the flames without harm. And the fourth is like the Son of God.'"

I stopped on the top stair, and waited. Now both his hands were over his head. His shadow curved and reached over the stairs' edge at my feet.

"Because when yo' in the fire, brotha — that is the Heart of God."

The door slammed behind me. I briefly thought of my finger tip on the floor of the men's dorm, but kept on moving. I did not know this then, but that was not all I was leaving behind.

I didn't acknowledge any of those who were smoking

or moving about in the alley as I went out, and then up West Street.

I crossed Tremont and there, just outside the Common, stood Stanley. He was in the same tee shirt with dried blood on the shoulder and had one arm wrapped around his chest. The other was held out to those who passed by him on their morning trek to the downtown office buildings and banks.

"Got any change sir? Got any change ma'm?" he chanted in a grave monotone. He didn't see me.

"Got any change, miss?" he said to a young girl with braids. She was in a plaid uniform and carried school books and, like most of the others who passed by, she ignored him.

I heard a voice from behind me and I turned to see Rosie sitting on the bench tying together a bundle of balloons to the corner of the nozzle on her helium tank.

"How was it that you can see them so clearly, but not yourself?" She didn't look up at me as she spoke.

"You were once without any blame, you know. You were a boy, too, with brothers and a baseball mitt. And I'm quite sure that you let them borrow that, or anything else, any time they wanted. Am I right?"

She scared me just then.

I entered the park, and started to run.

7:27 AM

Running up the Hill to my studio I'd anticipated a sense of relief or at least safety when I returned home. That slim hope vanished as I slid my key into the lock.

I leaned against the closing door and watched my chest rise and fall, waiting for it to catch up with the rest of me.

My apartment was one room, fifteen by thirty feet. On the wall to the right was a closet-size pantry. A small refrigerator sat beneath about four feet of counter space and a microwave with a dial that maxed at 30 minutes but would only cook for about five at a time. Wedged between three shelves and a single cabinet was a narrow window that the cupboard obscured by about six inches.

Beneath the only other window was my bed — an old beaten-up futon that used to spend the daylight hours as a couch but, in the time I'd spent in the studio, had remained opened and unmade, as if in a state of perpetual summons to me. The place came furnished with an old veneer dresser and a moth-eaten armchair. On the wall straight ahead stood a card table with two folding metal chairs.

My heart pounded against my ribs. Everything about the room — the air, the walls, and the furniture—was too close.

What's happening? Stepping over the dirty clothes I'd begun to gather and separate for the laundry four or five days before, I collapsed on my bed. I wiped at the warm tickle of sweat dripping down from my temples and reached for the clock-radio that sat on a box still packed full with books.

"Seven thirty-five," I said aloud, as if my declaration of the time, the concept of it, would somehow restore pieces of the scaffolding that was quickly dismantling beneath my feet. But the numbers didn't *mean* anything.

The pantry appeared shaded and cool; inviting even. Long spokes of sunlight shone through thin slits between the closed blinds, invading the room with a cruel intent, as though it pierced the comforting dimness to take something from me.

The light taunted me, and I realized that I'd never once raised those blinds.

I smelled something sweet and foul at the same time, like rotted fruit. I tried to think of the last time I'd had any in the house. *When the fuck did I...?*

I stood up; my legs felt rooted to the floor. I slowly realized that I was still in my jacket. I pulled at the zipper and slid it off, letting it fall on the bed behind me. I swallowed hard and it hurt, like something growing, expanding deep in my throat, and went into the pantry for a glass of water.

By the sink I was overtaken by the stench. *Why did I not smell this last night before I went to work, or the day before?*

I shuffled through the weeks of mail, emptied soda bottles and plastic bags on the counter. Then, hidden from view beneath a crumpled Styrofoam container and a Wendy's bag, I found three bananas inside a wooden bowl jammed between the oven and a Dewar's carton from my old restaurant, still filled with dishes. They were black and shrunken to the size of large vanilla beans and covered with nesting fruit flies that hovered over the bowl and swarmed when I picked it up.

I pushed the bowl deep inside an open, overstuffed green trash bag and some used paper napkins and coffee grounds spilled onto the floor. The bananas had attached themselves to the wood, and I just let go. I pulled the draw strings into a tight knot and went out my apartment door, leaving it wide open. I ran down all five flights and out to the sidewalk, the entire time holding the bag in front of me as one would grasp some fearsome creature and threw it in one of the barrels beside the front stoop, jamming the plastic lid down hard, pounding around the outside of it, making sure the rim was sealed on all sides.

Back inside my apartment, I slammed the door shut and leaned against it again.

Right. I was here a moment ago...

"Water," I said with authority, remembering where I'd left off. But I was compelled head for the pantry and throw open the blinds first. Dust flew into my mouth and nose. I closed my eyes as I pounded on the top sash of the window that had been painted shut long before I lived there. I gave up, fell back against the counter and watched the storms of settling dust rage in wide beams of invading light. The blocks of yellow linoleum on the floor that caught the sun were a different shade from what they had been, brighter than if I'd just washed them.

I shifted my weight on the counter from one arm to the other. I wasn't as short of breath anymore, but my heart still raced, and dust coated my mouth.

"Water!" I shouted this time.

The sink was full and I picked up a mug which had dribbles of coffee dried on the side, and ran it under cold water while rubbing the outside. While rinsing I absent-mindedly noted the mess on the counter. The debris was different too, somehow; as if exposed as something else in the bright sun.

I filled the cup and lifted it to my mouth. Before the water reached my lips, I saw a loose piece of floating mold move toward my mouth from the spot where it had slowly grown, and threw down the mug as though it had bitten my hand. I covered my face while pieces of pottery hit the counter and me.

Slowly, steadily, I took my hand away and surveyed the chaos around me with detachment. The room was no more disheveled than it had been before. Among the disarray, nothing was out of place.

What, then?

On top of a folded brown paper bag I saw a piece of the small white soufflé bowl from a set of my grandmother's. It had a big, handsome swan on the bottom and when I was small I thought it was the ugly duckling. That bowl was all I would eat from when visiting with my grandparents as a child, the only thing I wanted when my grandfather died and my grandmother went to live with my uncle's family in Connecticut.

Now it was shattered.

I wanted to be angry at myself, but I couldn't. It was simply one more thing that had been taken from me.

"I surrender," I said. Folding my arms, I lifted them to cover my eyes.

Silence...

I coughed again and the growing thickness in my throat made it nearly impossible to swallow. I tried with every muscle in my neck and jaws to suppress its swelling.

"If I keep it here, you see," I said to the empty room, "then it will stay in front of me, always, and not be trailing behind."

I remembered how I watched Mark's grave from the rear of the limousine as I left the cemetery that morning.

"It will stay right there, and not get smaller and smaller as I pull away."

Every muscle in my body ached. All I wanted to do was quench my thirst and lie down, but the sun now filled the room and seemed to usher me out. Dizzy, off-balance, a burning sour taste pushed up from my throat, and I leaned against the wall on my way into the bathroom.

I pressed one hand on the sink and turned on the cold water. At first my palm slipped on the rim from built-up soap and spattered toothpaste. I splashed at some of the chalky stains and tried to rub them away. I scooped up a small, cool pool of water in my good hand. It tasted sweet and felt so clean when I splashed my face then ran my cool, wet fingers through my hair.

In the mirror I looked flushed, glistening. The bluish sets of scars crisscrossing my wrist gleamed as well, almost violet from my exertion and the cool morning air. I caught my eyes in the cloudy mirror and shut them tightly.

A quiet buzz in the room, almost a hum seemed to emanate from all the little stitch marks on the inside of my arm, and they murmured quietly:

"See? We are the only precedence he set for his brother — the only one that stuck."

Letting the water splash into the sink, I reached up and put my hand beside the mirror while throwing all of my weight against the wall. My eyes were still clenched and I followed the negative images of the scars as they floated behind my eyelids. I searched for something within the drifting lines: Anything that might suggest that these marks were *not* all I ever gave my brother. They weren't the only things.

I opened my eyes and was instantly drawn back to my wrist, and then away again, to the mirror and the deep black of my pupils. I measured the ebony, then the blue around it, and then the bloodshot whites surrounding them. I pulled away a few inches. How heavily they peered back, full of a gravity that unveiled a part of me to which I was defenseless. I had no choice but to look.

The image of Stanley's eyes, enormous and deep brown, came to me, and for an instant the same rush of deep empathy coursed through me as had earlier that morning when I'd cleaned his face.

Then Stanley's eyes were gone and it was Sampson's all-too-knowing, but still innocently questioning, wide baby blues staring, and as I began to scrutinize them with a keen sense of sorrow mixed with awe, they vanished as well. I was left with only my own, watching back from the same sink, inside an identical reflected room.

I could almost hear Rosie as though she were right beside me, *"They are your eyes, Mr. Julien."*

"They're mine?"

And it was as if she were answering me, clear as day, and I heard her last words to me from the sidewalk on my way home, *"How is it that you can see them so plainly, but not yourself?"*

"I don't know!" I said out loud.

"You were a boy once, too, with brothers and a baseball mitt." She said, *"And I'm quite sure that you let them borrow that, or anything else, any time they wanted. Am I right?"*

"Yes," I said emphatically, trying to drive home the point, for her, for me. Then I thought of Stanley on the floor hallucinating, believing I was *his* brother, and it came to me again: he was a little kid once, before anything happened to him, before he had any blame. I could see that. But so was I...

What boy ever chased after a ball, or delivered a newspaper, or ordered his brother not to wheel a carriage too fast?

I let my arms drop beside me.

Then I remembered something I'd seemed to have forgotten a long time before. I saw myself as I had coming out of that other time in my life, the drunken, blurry haze that began to clear one morning while I was strapped to a hospital bed. When I awoke to find myself in a place that I didn't choose; when I first realized that I had a role, just like everyone else. But I hadn't written parts of that script; I had no control over them then, or now.

"Thank you, you old wine-soaked, crazy bag lady." I said in a hoarse whisper, "Thank you."

Silence...

All at once it was as if I'd been absolved of a secret lie I'd been tricked into keeping. In return, some strange beauty had been revealed to me — again: *I'm just a player too.*

So very blue my eyes were now. So bright and clear were the whites that bordered them that they reminded me of Kodachrome snapshots taken of me when I was small.

My heart pounded and I knew the choice to stop its beating was not mine. It never was — no more than I could simply will it to stop racing at that moment.

How could it have been Mark's decision?

"But I'm still here," I said.

Collapsing on my futon, I wasn't even thinking of sleep. I lay there for a while. Then I sat up, and pulled my shirt and sweater over my head and a rippling coolness spread over damp areas of my back.

Now, I know something about what a reptile might feel when shedding its worn-out, no-longer-needed skin.

But there was something else I knew.

Since Mark had died I'd cried only sparingly, with the conscious fear that one day the tears would stop, and along with them would leave the part of me that included him. But now I could see that what I had left within me, that which included Mark, couldn't be used up, and I let them all go.

I felt as though my heart's blood were being drained from me. Everything inside me sank and swam. I had the sensation that something was pushing on my chest, and looked down expecting to see my fingers pressing against my left ribcage, but didn't. Instinctively my hand was drawn there anyway and remained in the same protective grasp, long after it ached from the position.

Exhausted, weary, but restless too, I felt a slow stirring deep within, as if the marrow in the very center of my bones were moving slightly; rearranging. I lay there for a very long time. My face was dry, my sheets only faintly damp when I began to fade into sleep.

Silence...

12:42 PM

While I slept the sunlight crept through the window and inched across the floor of my studio, my bed. The air was warm, almost hot. I ached to turn over and slip back into unconsciousness, but sat up on the side of my bed. My loosely bandaged hand began to throb. I had the overwhelming urge to get up and out of my apartment.

1:08 PM

When I reached the bottom of the Hill, Charles Street was full of people on their lunch hour, searching for a place to sit or a cafe that had broken out the sidewalk furniture early for the season. Doors and windows were open to restaurants and shops. Luncheon special boards were written in brightly colored chalk, and signs boasting Spring Savings dotted the brick and cobblestone sidewalks.

Everything was out of the ordinary, but not unfamiliar. Just brighter and more defined, as if I'd been returned from a long absence.

I closely watched each face I passed: An Asian woman in a green dress, a pair of teenage girls, arm in arm, both laughing, a kid on roller blades with headphones, another dude a bit older, with a brown buzz-cut and a stern expression. I was at ease, yet in awe of the day and the people and the sounds

Could they see what I saw?

1:12 PM

Moving briskly from side to side along the crowded sidewalk to the end of the street, I crossed over Beacon. Beside the entrance of the ornate wrought-iron fence that surrounded the Public Garden I waited for the flood of mid-day strollers to exit the park. The air, warm and sweet, was rich with the ground's first thaw. I closed my eyes for a moment in the shade of a giant oak tree as I waited.

I didn't know where I was headed, but I don't remember ever being more aware of such a deep sense of beauty. I felt that a natural order had returned; all the planets were momentarily lined up and in that instant I saw a fleeting glimpse of how everything was constant, and important, and happening all at once. I was exactly where I was supposed to be.

1:21 PM

I stopped along the pathway beside the green spears of crocus and tulip bulbs reaching through the soil. There were children everywhere and I wondered if it were a school vacation. Farther up I saw an empty bench and walked toward it.

I sat there for a long time, eyes closed, head back, and did not want to move. I consumed every gust of mild air as I would sweet syrup, and all that was going on around me seemed to be permeated with a quiet ease.

The pathways were not silent, or the streets, or the city. But somewhere inside all bewilderment, injury and torment had suddenly ceased, and all else was placed back under my control.

After some time I opened my eyes and sat up straight. I was ready for more sleep but remembered that I needed to call Carey and took out my cell. He was already at work.

"What's up?"

"*What's up?*" he said back, as if the term made no sense.

"I called you," I said.

He was silent for a moment, then, cynically, "Ah, yeah?"

"I *told* you I would call you back this morning."

"Ah yeah," he said again, but this time lighter in sarcasm, not pissed off at me at all as was usual of late. "You haven't called me back in over year, dude. Forgive me if I am a bit taken back."

This time I had nothing to say.

"What *is* up?" he said, "How did your night go?"

"Oh, Man. I wouldn't even know where to begin… What are you doing later?"

"What do you mean?"

"I mean, do you want to get together? Maybe grab a bite or something. Catch up."

"Well," he stumbled a bit. "Hell-yeah. That'd be so great. It's been too long."

"Want me to come by your place? Is about seven good?"

"That's perfect," I said.

"Promise me you will be there."

"Oh, I'll be there," I said quietly, then to myself, "in spades."

"In what?"

"Oh, nothing. Also, tell me again: What did Terry say when you saw her at the restaurant?"

"That your job is still waiting for you. And that they opened the new place in Copley. She said they could really use help getting things running smoothly over there. You should call her."

"I think I just might give her a shout," I paused. "There was something else I called you about."

"Oh, what now?" he said, the cynicism making a slight return. "I knew this was too good to be true."

"Oh, relax."

"Is that the other reason you called me? To tell me to relax?"

"No… I… Well, I wanted to say…"

"Say what?"

"That I'm sorry. Really."

"O.K..," he said, "For what?"

"For being so fucking concerned about myself, I guess. So much so that… I don't know. But I totally missed that …" I fumbled for words.

"Missed what? Dude, I think you need some sleep.

You're not making any sense."

"I didn't know you were scared," I said loudly, over him. "That's not me, and you know that. But I'm sorry."

I could hear Carey breathing, and ambient office sounds of chatter and doors in the background from his end.

Finally, I said, "I'm scared too, sometimes. But I got this, O.K.?"

"O.K.," he said, as though he believed me.

"And this is going to pass. For the both of us, I mean. I promise."

"That's cool, Bro." He said. "It's all good. But thanks for saying that. I appreciate it. And I know this is not you. Julien's favorite subject was never Julien. It was always everyone else first, especially Mark and me. Do you think I don't know that? "

He said that he had to get back to work and would see me at seven, and hung up.

I wanted to rally the energy to make my way back up the Hill to my place, but stayed where I was for a bit.

A young couple was sitting closely to one another by the side of the pond. They had their shoes off and pant legs rolled up while they dipped their pale feet just beneath the surface. Then I turned to the sound of a woman's stern voice coming from a bench nearby.

About forty years old, she stood beside the bench directly across from mine. She rocked a large blue canvas carriage with one hand, had the other on her hip.

"Matthew," she said again, in a stronger tone, "Get over here and watch your brother — *Now!*"

Fifty feet beyond, a boy of about twelve was passing a basketball back and forth with a friend. The two stood on the edge of the courts, which were overrun with older boys playing shirts and skins. He turned toward the woman, shook his head, spit, and kicked up a small cloud of dirt. He caught the ball one last time before walking to her.

She took his hand and placed it on the handle without

interrupting her already steady bounce of the carriage. Then he sat on the ball, while rocking the carriage, and watched her walk away with a scowl on his face. He stretched to look inside, and stuck his free hand in as if to adjust something.

I closed my eyes once more, and all was still silent.

I opened them in time to see the woman return to relieve him of his vigil. He ran back to the court where the older kids were now done. His friends were just beginning to choose sides.

He hadn't missed a thing.

Silence...

"O I am not afraid, my voices! You shall be very proud of me, for I shall be very beautiful for you: I will dress myself carefully in thick red fire and in sharp white fire and in cool blue fire. Now it is not dark and there is no world: perfectly begins to grow a brighter brightness than all of the sky and of the sea and of the earth;

"...Now all the little flames are lifting me higher than tomorrow in all of their hands — Man Who Is God! Take from these alive fingers on shining bird" ~ e.e. cummings

Epilogue

I never did get my finger looked at, but it healed just fine; took a little while, that's all. If you look close you can see the tip is a bit lop-sided and the nail doesn't grow evenly across. Otherwise you wouldn't notice. But if I bump it, even lightly, it hurts like it probably should have that night.

When I look back and see myself sitting there in the park that day, I remember how it was also on a city bench, across the street in The Common, where Rosie died of sunstroke one blazing afternoon the following July.

There was a small article in The Globe that told of a standing-room-only memorial service in the church over the shelter, of which I unfortunately had no knowledge. The cop who found her was quoted in the paper as saying: "I passed her about three times late in the afternoon and thought she was just snoozing. No one would bother Rosie. Not unless it was getting really cold outside, or dark."

It was at dusk when he tried to rouse her, and realized she was gone. Sometimes I speculate if she'll present herself to me again, and whether or not I will know her.

Was Rosie a goddess, or a hag? I knew she was a mother once and wanted to be a teacher and grow tomatoes. But would I have been able to see myself in the mirror — truly see myself as *just a player* — if I had not bestowed that kiss upon her cheek?

END

*Please support this author by reviewing **Kissing the Hag** on your favorite book website(s), and by telling your friends about the book. Thank you.*

Addenda

ABOUT TIMOTHY QUIGLEY

Timothy Quigley's award-winning stories have appeared in *The Chariton Review, Line Zero Journal of Art and Literature, La Ostra Magazine, Writer's World*, as well as various online publications. He is also the screenwriter of two short films; one animated, and the other a live action adapted from one of his short stories. He is currently working on a feature-length film adaptation of *Kissing the Hag*, as well as a collection of short stories. Quigley received his MFA in Writing from Vermont College of Norwich University, and currently teaches writing and literature at Salem State University and Wentworth Institute in Boston.

Connect with Timothy at Twitter: @timquq, LinkedIn: Timothy Quigley, facebook.com/quigtim, or TimothyQuigley.org.

ACKNOWLEDGEMENTS

A very special thanks to all of the members in every writing workshop in which I have ever participated from Boston to Yale to Vermont to Hazel Street, as well as boundless gratitude to all of my writing mentors who, through their generosity and commitment, allowed me to grow as a writer, and to find and believe in my own voice: Jane Barnes, Christopher Tilghman, Carol Anshaw, Sharon Sheehe Stark and Bret Lott. To all of my family and friends, you know who you are: you have always believed in me a bit more than I ever did in myself and, without every one of you, this would never have been possible.

And deep appreciation to Sally Wiener Grotta, Daniel Grotta, and Frank Wilson for trusting in this book and working so hard to see it on the shelves.

Timothy Quigley

ABOUT PIXEL HALL PRESS

Pixel Hall Press (www.PixelHallPress.com) is a relatively new, old-fashioned small publishing house that focuses on discovering literary gems and great stories that might have otherwise been overlooked. Our mission is to publish books that energize the imagination and intrigue the mind, and to be a conduit between readers and provocative, stimulating, talented authors.

Please go to the For Readers & Book Clubs section of the Pixel Hall Press website, to find out about various programs we offer readers. These include free Study Guides for book discussion leaders, our Beta Reader program which offers access to free pre-publication eBooks, and the Author Connect Program which helps to set up book discussions with our authors for reading groups. We also have volume discounts on books for discussion groups, organizations and classrooms.

Join in on the discussion about books, reading, writing and the publishing industry on Pixel Hall Press's Facebook page and on Twitter: @PixelHallPress.